SECRET DREAMS

by
C. Mercedes Wilson

To Nancy,
all my best

C Mercedes Wilson

Secret Dreams
by C. Mercedes Wilson
Published by Blue Tulip Publishing
www.bluetulippublishing.com

To Phil: you bring out the best in me

CHAPTER ONE

June 15, 2015

JULIA METCALF AWOKE UNABLE TO BREATHE. Her limbs jolted in four different directions as though she were being electrocuted. She gasped for air, frantically scanning her surroundings. As her brain began to recognize the familiar objects in her room, her breathing resumed and the pounding in her chest subsided.

In a flash, she grabbed the journal from her bedside table and began scribbling as many details of the dream as she could remember. A gentle night breeze rippled the lace curtains as she settled back on the flowered pillows.

As she wrote, her vital signs gradually returned to normal, but she couldn't shake the feeling that something was very wrong.

I was in the woods, she wrote. *It was twilight, and I couldn't see very well. There were shadows everywhere. Strange moaning and howling sounds came from all directions. I peered into the thicket as hard as I could, but I wasn't able to see where the noises came from.*

Suddenly, a dark veil appeared to take over the forest, creeping nearer. I knew I had to get home as fast as I could. I ran and ran, but the blackness was catching up...

I looked over my shoulder and saw a tiny speck of light in the inky sky. It looked like a firefly. I had to rescue it because of that summer when Mae and I caught a whole bunch of them and kept them in a jar. Something inside me was inexplicably drawn to help the poor little thing lost in all of that gloom.

I turned and started to make my way back. A cold wind sliced at me, impeding my progress, and the shadowy veil enveloped me. I raised my arm to guard my face against the debris that began to pelt me as I trudged toward the speck. I couldn't see anything at all except that tiny bit of light, and I tripped over something that felt like brambles. They bit at my shins and ankles. I kept going, and at last I was close enough to stretch an arm toward the speck.

Gently, I closed my hand over it, just as Mae and I did with the fireflies, and turned. "Hold on tight," I whispered as I started toward home. The shadows had no end, and there seemed no way back to the forest, so I sat down with my back to the freezing wind. Shielding my fist with my body, I slowly opened my hand.

My heart caught in my throat, and my hands shook. I dropped the speck. It flew back to me as the gloom seemed to wane slightly and it hovered before my eyes. It was Mae. "Help me, Julia," she said. "It's so dark, and I didn't want to come. I think they're going to hurt me." Then she faded into the shadows.

Suddenly, it hit Julia. Mae was in serious trouble. She dropped her pen and picked up her phone. She scooped her long, silver-streaked blonde hair over her shoulder and hit her speed dial with shaking fingers. When she didn't get an answer, she tried the house phone.

"Yeah?" a male voice answered.

"Seth?"

"Julia?" Mae's stepson replied as though bored.

"What happened?" Tears were tracking down her face as

she waited for his reply.

"What are you talking about?"

"Mae's in trouble. Go see if she's all right," Julia demanded, pacing as she spoke.

A few moments passed, and Seth came back to the phone.

"She's gone, and her room is trashed."

There was no concern in his voice, but Julia trembled in fear. She breathed slowly and deeply until she felt reasonably in control.

"Okay, did you hear or see anything?"

"No, I just got home."

"Call the police, and don't go in her room. I'll be there in a few."

"Whatever."

She could never tell for sure what the dreams meant, which was why she wrote them down. Sometimes their message was clear, and other times the visions were very cryptic. Her bedroom bookshelves were lined with journals, each dated and numbered in Julia's deliberate hand.

She threw on a pair of jeans and a sweatshirt, and then twisted her hair into a haphazard braid. With her journal under one arm and her purse under the other, Julia ran out of the house and threw open the door on her SUV. The damp midnight air seeped into her bones. She wished she'd grabbed a jacket and some socks instead of shoving her feet into her mules and hurrying out the door.

She slammed the vehicle into reverse and floored it. In record time, Julia covered the two and a half miles to Mae's exclusive neighborhood. With shaking fingers, she carefully pressed her code into the security pad at the gate of the Arbeson estate. The tires squealed as Julia careened up the circular drive. The suspension groaned in protest as she hit the brakes at the portico near the front door. The SUV had hardly stopped moving before Julia was out and running for the door.

CHAPTER TWO

JULIA JARVIS METCALF AND MAE LANGFORD ARBESON had been friends since childhood. At the age of eight, they met at the park near the Langford estate. Mae's governess, Nell, used to take the child for long walks to help curb her energy. The family made their fortune when Richard Langford sold a large parcel of Alaskan land for the pipeline. They had two children. Eddy was six years older than Mae. Nell took care of young Mae and loved her as her own. Eddy had proclaimed himself too old for a governess, and the Langfords allowed him the freedom to choose so long as he conducted himself in a responsible fashion.

Julia and Mae met daily at the park for several weeks. Julia's mother, a self-proclaimed hippie, publicly detested everything Mae's family represented. Privately, she was happy that Julia had some of the advantages that wealth provided. She could see that the two girls connected on a deep level. Julia was often invited to stay at the Langford's estate.

She and Mae grew as close as sisters. When Mae lost her

temper, she threw everything she could get her hands on. Julia supposed it started as her way of getting attention from her parents. Nell tried fervently to talk her down, but ultimately, Julia was the only one to whom Mae would listen when a tantrum dominated her — it was something she never really outgrew.

Mae bawled her eyes out to Julia when Tommy Peterson broke her heart by dumping her after two weeks for Molly O'Reilly. It seemed so horrible then, so scandalous that he'd do such a thing, but they were ten; they knew nothing of real heartbreak.

When Julia went steady for the first time, they were fourteen; it was Mae who stroked Julia's hair after the three-month whirlwind romance was cut short when George McGregor's incessant jealousy proved to be too much for Julia to bear. Julia had thought the relationship would last forever, but decided the thought of forever wasn't so pleasant when each day a new imagined rival sparked George's rage.

Now Julia and Mae would laugh about both incidents. Twenty-some years later, Tommy was a raging alcoholic. Poor George was dead before they even graduated high school. *Why is it that high school boys always think themselves invincible, especially when riding on a motorcycle without a helmet?*

Julia still shuddered from the thought. She'd dreamt about George that night. But back then she was less confident that her dreams really told her anything. George's accident was a turning point for Julia; after that she didn't doubt her dreams when they told her something was amiss.

In 1995, upon the eve of Julia's marriage to her ex, Jeffrey Metcalf, Mae pulled Julia aside. "Jule, I don't know about Jeff."

"You're telling me this now? What do you mean?"

Mae tilted her head full of gorgeous brown curls and held Julia's hands. "You know what I mean."

At the time, Julia was angry. *How could Mae do this on the night before my wedding?* "He loves me Mae. It's going to work out just fine."

Mae had smiled and hugged Julia and said nothing more.

Unlike Jeff, Mae was there to hold Julia's hand through her many miscarriages. After the first one in early 1997, Mae and her steady date, millionaire Harvey Arbeson, insisted upon Julia and Jeff meeting them at the club for dinner. The evening cheered Julia immeasurably until just after the dessert course, when Harvey dropped to one knee. Julia thought him a pompous jerk, but it was clear that he loved Mae dearly.

"Mae darling, you know I have deep feelings for you."

What? You're going to propose, and you can't even say you love her? Julia thought. Mae's hands were shaking so Julia gave one a comforting squeeze.

"I can't live without you," he proclaimed. He looked up into her eyes. "Marry me?"

No, don't do it. He was ten years Mae's senior, and it was Julia's opinion that he merely wanted a trophy wife.

He flashed his brilliantly white dental veneers and Mae melted.

"Yes of course, Harv."

Harvey slipped an obnoxiously large stone on Mae's finger and kissed her hand.

The entire membership of the club stood and applauded while Mae turned bright red and grinned. Julia smiled too, but inside, her heart hurt.

Upon leaving the club, the foursome waited while Harvey spoke to the valet. He winked and slipped an arm around Mae's shoulders. A moment later, the valet pulled up in a beautiful 1955 Thunderbird convertible.

"Oh look, Harv. Isn't it wonderful? I'm more than a bit jealous of whoever owns that beauty." Mae looked at it longingly.

"I think I recognize it, and I believe I know the owner."

Harvey's eyes lit up.

"You do? What I wouldn't give for a ride." Mae scanned her surroundings for the owner.

"Darling, if I might have your attention for just a moment?"

"Of course, Harv."

"I have a little engagement present for you." He handed her an envelope.

She smiled up at him and opened it. Suddenly, her mouth dropped open and the color drained from her face.

"Mae," Julia said. "What's wrong?"

"It's the title to the Thunderbird." Her hands shook. A girlish giggle started deep inside, and bubbled up to a near shriek. She threw her arms around Harvey. "Oh Harv, she's mine? She's really mine?" Mae smothered his face with kisses.

"Mae," Harvey said quietly. "Stop. You're quite forgetting yourself. We talked about this. Propriety at all times."

Mae suddenly stopped and lowered her eyes. "I'm sorry." A smile grew across her face. "I just couldn't help myself."

"It's all right, Darling. I know it's a bit overwhelming. I'll let it pass, just this once."

What a jerk. Julia wanted to yank Mae away from him and forbid her to ever lay eyes on him again.

The date was set for June 29, 1998. The wedding would rival that of the royal family. As matron of honor, it was Julia's responsibility and right to plan the shower and the bachelorette party, but Harvey wouldn't hear of it. He assigned his social secretary, Marilyn, to make all the arrangements — including the bridal shower. The only thing Mae was allowed to choose was her wedding gown. A bachelorette party was out of the question.

Of course, Harvey spent the eve of their wedding at the club, undoubtedly with many of his male friends, not having a stag party. *Yeah, right.* Mae spent it sharing a bottle of

7

champagne and a large bowl of strawberries with her sister of the heart.

On the morning of the wedding, Julia felt like a street urchin next to the very wealthy and snobbish. She paced outside while Marilyn helped Mae prepare.

"The hell with this," Julia said out loud and barged in. "Mae, I need a minute of your undivided attention."

"Not now," Marilyn interrupted. "We're running late."

Julia whirled to face her. "Back off. I'm the matron of honor and want a moment with the bride. Do you have a problem with that?" Fire burned in the pit of her stomach.

Marilyn stared a moment. "Marilyn, it's okay," Mae said gently. "They're not going to start without us."

Marilyn backed out of the room and shut the door quietly.

"I really want to punch her."

Mae laughed. "What is it, Jule? Did you have another dream?"

"No." She sat down. "Mae, are you okay with all of this?"

"What do you mean?"

"Well… Harvey. He's just so, I don't know. Full of himself?"

Mae sat next to Julia and put an arm around her. "When I was a little girl, Nellie used to tell me I was a princess and someday, I would marry a prince. As I grew older, she would tell me that while marrying a prince was all well and good in a fairy tale, real men were imperfect. They'd often think of themselves first. I was always expected to marry someone of equal or greater social standing. It was my duty. Are you asking if I love Harv?"

Julia nodded.

"Yes Jule, I do. Is it perfect? Is he perfect? No, on both counts. But, he brings a lot into this marriage just as I do. He's appointing me to the board of the foundation." She smiled.

The Arbeson Foundation provided select charities huge contributions. Mae would help decide how much and to whom the money would go.

Julia put a hand on Mae's cheek. "As long as you're happy..."

"I'm fine, Jule."

"Okay."

A moment later, Marilyn knocked on the door and opened it without waiting for a response. "We really must begin. Everyone is waiting." She glanced nervously at her watch.

Mae took Julia's hand. "Come on, let's get in line. We can talk while the twelve bridesmaids start up the aisle." Her musical laugh filled the air.

"Can we gossip and whisper nasty things about everyone?"

"Perfect! You start."

"Fine. I'll wait until you get back from your honeymoon." She plastered on a fake pout and Mae kissed her cheek in response.

Julia slowly walked up the aisle on the arm of the best man. He was an attractive middle-aged oil baron from Texas. Jeff's distrust showed in the scathing look he shot at Julia from his seat in the cathedral. She prayed he would stay somewhat sober at the reception.

Mae's train was fifteen feet of the softest silk available. It seemed to float behind her, not that anyone noticed. Her glowing face outshone the flowers, the gown, the sweeps of tulle, and the entire wedding party. Harvey's gaze never wavered from his beautiful bride.

When at long last Mae arrived at the altar, he took her hand and kissed it affectionately. The archbishop was a personal friend and considered it an honor to preside.

The ceremony made Julia cry, both for its beauty and for

what she thought Mae was giving up.

The reception was attended by 1,600 of Harvey and Mae's acquaintances. It took well over three hours for the guests to file past the receiving line. Julia's feet had turned against her. She fervently hoped she would not have to dance with anyone.

When the wedding party took their places at the head table, the caterers seemed to multiply as the first of seven courses was served. The sumptuous meal left Julia feeling overfull and lethargic.

Marilyn had outdone herself. The orchestra played "I Only Have Eyes For You," as Harvey guided Mae across the dance floor. No one knew better than Julia how much Mae detested the spotlight, and dancing. But she smiled through the entire ordeal, her gaze riveted on her new husband.

Jeff sat sullenly throughout the affair. Julia chose to view that as a good thing. At least he was quiet and relatively sober.

The following morning, the new Mr. and Mrs. Arbeson left for an exclusive European honeymoon. It was the longest month of Julia's life.

On the morning of their return, Mae called Julia, rousing her from sleep. "Mae? Are you okay?"

"I have so much to tell you. Come over for coffee."

CHAPTER THREE

June 15, 2015

JULIA POUNDED ON THE ORNATELY CARVED oak door. A security car pulled up behind her, illuminating the portico under which she stood.

The guard sauntered over to her. "Excuse me. I assume you don't have an appointment at this hour?" He rested his hand on his pepper spray. His rumpled uniform and bloodshot eyes revealed his less than fastidious work ethic.

"Mrs. Arbeson is my best friend, and something has happened to her."

"Like what?" He eyed her torn jeans and sloppy sweatshirt suspiciously.

"I just talked to her stepson, and he told me that she is gone and her room is trashed."

"Well, he didn't call me, and if something like that happened, I'd think he would have. This is a private estate, and you can't go knocking on doors in the middle of the night."

Julia's face reddened and her lips pursed. She put a hand on her hip. She'd had enough of this wannabe policeman. "Watch me," she replied, resuming her pounding.

"If you don't get off this property right now, I'm calling the police."

Julia turned and stared at him. "How do you think I got past the gate, Einstein? I have my own code, and I let myself in."

"Ma'am." The guard took a step toward her as Seth finally opened the heavy door, chewing on part of the sandwich cradled in his hand.

"It's all right, I know her," he said to the guard as Julia stepped inside and shut the door behind her.

"New guy," Seth explained as he turned around and headed for the kitchen.

"Did you call the police?"

"Yeah, but they said I can't report her missing yet. She's only been gone a couple of hours. She was here when I left to go out with my friends," he said while chewing.

"What about her room?" Julia inquired, heading for the back staircase.

Seth followed her up the stairs. "See for yourself."

Julia pushed open the door and looked in. The suite was in shambles. The bedclothes were strewn over the floor, one of the table lamps was overturned, and the mirror outside the bathroom door was smashed. The size and configuration of the rooms prevented her from seeing the small details, but she resisted the urge to go in and touch the things that were out of place.

"Well, go on in," Seth said.

"No," she replied. "The police will want to process this as a crime scene."

"I told you, they said they wouldn't come." He shifted from foot to foot. "I guess we'll have to figure it out for ourselves." He stole a glance Julia's way. Something in his eyes disturbed her deeply. Could he have had something to do with this? The thought angered her.

"The hell they aren't." Julia pulled out her cell and called 911.

CHAPTER FOUR

August 1, 1998

MAE POURED COFFEE INTO A DAINTY flowered china cup and handed it to Julia.

"Jule, you'd adore the Louvre. I spent three whole days just wandering through."

"I've heard it's not to be missed."

Mae sipped her tea.

"What is it? Something isn't right."

She set down her cup. "Come with me."

Julia followed her upstairs and Mae swung open the door to the nursery.

"Good afternoon, Mrs. Arbeson." The au pair nodded to Julia. A dark haired toddler played with a colorful set of wooden blocks.

"Who is he?" Julia asked.

"It was in Paris that Harv told me about Seth."

Julia waited quietly. Mae smiled and waved at the boy then shut the door. They walked slowly back to the parlor.

After a moment, Mae recounted the story.

"'You have a son?' I asked. 'Why didn't you tell me?'

"Then Harvey looked away before he replied. 'I don't know. He's a fine boy. Full of life and spirit.'

"I told him he sounded wonderful and I'd be happy to be his new mommy. I grinned and took Harvey's hand. Then he said something sad. 'Don't worry too much about it. His au pair takes care of the unpleasant parts. Diapers and such.' So I asked him if the au pair loved him. He looked at me as though I had two heads. It took him a moment to reply. 'I suppose, in some way.'

"Jule, I swear. I didn't know until he told me at that lovely little sidewalk café in Paris."

Julia scowled. "Why the hell didn't he tell you? Don't you think a previous marriage and a child are important things to discuss?"

"Well, yes. I'll give you that."

"So what happened?"

"He wasn't actually married to her."

"What?"

"He tells people that it was a whirlwind romance and elopement that was quickly annulled when his parents found out. He tells everyone that they didn't approve of her. She had no social standing."

"I am sick and tired of this what-do-the-neighbors-think mentality."

"It's easier this way."

"What's the real story?"

"The mother was a servant and agreed to keep her mouth shut if the child was afforded a first class upbringing. She lives in Switzerland. Harv agreed so long as she never darkened his door again. She terminated all rights and Seth will be told that she died when he's old enough to understand."

Julia shook her head.

"Excuse me, Miss Mae?" Elsa, the maid, poked her head

into the parlor.

"Yes?"

"Mr. Arbeson is waiting for you. He is ready to leave."

"Oh! I forgot. We have a charity luncheon." She jumped up and kissed Julia on the cheek. "Gotta run."

MAE AND JULIA SAT in the nursery on many occasions. They were never allowed much time; Harvey kept Mae on a tight social schedule.

One day, when Seth was about five, he began pounding a wooden block on Mae's knee.

"Stop that, Seth. You're hurting me."

He looked her square in the eye and pounded harder.

Mae grabbed his hand. "I said, stop it."

He bit the base of her thumb so hard, blood flowed almost immediately.

"Seth! Stop!" Mae's cries were frantic.

He bit down harder. Julia reached over and pinched the back of his thigh as hard as she could. He screamed, but released his hold on Mae.

Harvey stood in the doorway to the nursery, shocked.

"The little brat bit her. I think she needs stitches." Julia held tight to Mae's hand to stop the bleeding.

Seth ran to his father and hugged his legs, frightened.

Harvey rubbed the boy's head and looked accusingly at Mae.

"Where's the au pair? What's her name again?"

"I gave Helen a break," Mae replied.

"He's her job. Yours is at my side. Am I understood?"

He's mad at Mae? Julia kept her mouth shut with great difficulty. "What about Mae's hand? I'll drive her to the emergency room."

Mae's blouse was spattered with blood. Harvey crossed the room and held out his hands. "Let me see."

Julia released the pressure for a moment and tears rolled down Mae's face.

"I'll call Roger."

Roger Eisenberg was their physician and a friend. He arrived within moments. Quietly and calmly, he cleaned and sutured the wound then gave Mae a tetanus shot and some antibiotics. He nodded to Harvey and left without as much as a goodbye.

Mae wasn't allowed to speak of the incident, nor was Seth disciplined for his actions. It made Julia's blood boil.

The boy was raised by nannies. The Arbesons went through a number of them. They were also not allowed to discipline him. Harvey felt it was not necessary for a boy of his social standing.

At fourteen, a drunken Seth took Mae's Thunderbird out for a spin and rear ended another vehicle. He left the scene laying rubber. Harvey hurried to accident site where the victim awaited a tow truck and the police. He was paid off before the police arrived. Again, no consequences for Seth.

"Harv, what are we going to do about Seth?" Mae asked when he returned.

"Darling, it's just a phase. The boy will grow out of it."

Just before Seth's sixteenth birthday, Harvey suffered a fatal heart attack. His will stipulated that Mae be given a generous stipend, and the rest was to be left in trust for Seth. Mae was left with the responsibility of administering the trust until such time as Seth had reached majority and had proven himself responsible. Since Mae was the sole heir to the Langford estate, she had no need of Harvey's money, and put her stipend back into the Arbeson Trust.

Julia recalled that since his eighteenth birthday, Seth

pushed ceaselessly for access, but Mae knew her stepson, and wisely held the account under strict observation. The young heir constantly badgered her about releasing control to him. After all, he was an adult.

June 15, 2015
SETH WAS UNAWARE OF Julia's gift — or curse, depending on the circumstances. It wasn't that they kept it a secret; it was just that he was incredibly self absorbed, and simply wasn't interested.

"I'll bet she just had one of her tantrums and left," Seth remarked. "But if you want to make an idiot of yourself and push it, be my guest."

She had to give that point to the kid. Mae did have her share of tantrums, but they were few and far between now and only happened when she was pushed to the end of her endurance.

Julia scowled as he turned his back.

"911, what is your emergency?" the dispatcher said.

"My friend is missing, and I'm afraid she may have been kidnapped," she began.

"How long has your friend been gone?"

"Not long, but she went to bed some time ago, and now she's not there, and her room has been ransacked. I didn't go in but I think I saw some spots that may have been blood."

The last statement was a lie, but certainly far more believable than "I had this dream..."

CHAPTER FIVE

March 31, 1992

GROWING UP, THEY WERE ALWAYS AT Mae's. Mae not only had her own room, she had every toy she ever wanted and then some, an indoor swimming pool, and servants galore. Julia grew up in a one-bedroom apartment that she shared with her mother. The one bedroom was her mother's. Julia's was a fold out couch in the living room.

She loved to visit the Langford estate, but Mae lamented that hers was a complicated life. She always had to dress just so, and act just so, and go to special schools so she could grow up just so. Mae commented that it was "just so" her parents could show her off as their little toy, and then send her to her room when they tired of her.

Of course, Mae knew about her friend's gift. Julia had been born with it. Her intuition served her well in always knowing what to say to Mae to encourage or soothe her, but it wasn't until they were about fourteen that Mae found out.

They were having a sleepover at the estate when in the

middle of the night, Julia sat bolt upright and screamed.

Mae shook her to wake her while yelling, "What's wrong? What's wrong?"

"In the pool!" Julia screamed. "In the pool!"

Mae ran to the next room and woke up her governess, Nell.

"Nelly," Mae whispered.

"What is it, child?" Nell replied.

"Nelly, Jule had a bad dream about the pool. Will you go with us so that I can show her that it's all right? Like you used to do for me when I had monsters under my bed?"

"Good lord, child," Nell began, but saw the worry on Mae's face. "All right. Let me get my robe." She shuffled into slippers and tied her robe as they crossed to Mae's room. Julia was still on the bed, curled up in a ball weeping.

"Why me?" she lamented. "Why do I have to dream this stuff? I'm too young."

"It's all right, Miss Julia." Nell rubbed her back and spoke in soothing tones. She and Mae coaxed her to come with them so she could see that it was just a dream.

"But it's not all right, don't you see?" Julia whined.

They patted her and nodded, knowing she was just frightened by the nightmare. As they opened the door to the indoor pool room, Nell stopped dead in her tracks, blocking the doorway with her generously proportioned frame.

"You girls wait out here," she demanded over her shoulder. She closed the door firmly. Next they heard a splash, and lots of watery noises. Then they heard Nell shout. "Girls?"

They cracked open the door and peeked in. Nell was giving mouth to mouth to Eddie, Mae's older brother. "Call the police, and tell them to get an ambulance here quick," she said between breaths.

Mae ran for the phone and dialed, quickly explaining what happened. Then she woke her parents. Later, after Eddie had been taken away by the coroner, Mae and Julia sat in her room.

"How did you know?" Mae asked amid her tears. Julia wrapped her arms around her friend and drew a deep breath.

"I had this dream," Julia replied.

"You dreamt he was drowning?" Mae pulled away only far enough to look Julia in the eye.

"Something like that."

"Do you dream stuff like that a lot?"

"Sometimes." Julia looked away. "I mean, I don't dream about any useful stuff like the answers to tomorrow's test or anything, but sometimes I just... see stuff in my dreams. It doesn't make sense most of the time."

"That's spooky. But it's also really cool. Well, not tonight, but you know."

"Mae, don't tell anybody, okay? I already feel like a freak."

"Cross my heart."

Julia felt as though an enormous weight had been lifted from her shoulders that night. Mae knew now. She didn't judge or make Julia feel like an outcast.

CHAPTER SIX

JULIA PACED UNTIL THE POLICE ARRIVED. Seth let them in and explained that the servants were off for the night and that Julia had insisted they be called.

How can that little shit be so calm? She thought.

"Ma'am?" a policeman said, addressing Julia.

She beckoned them up the stairs to Mae's room.

"Does this strike you as at all odd?" she asked as the door swung open.

"Whoa," the young cop remarked. He spoke into his radio asking for a detective and the crime lab.

The next several hours were a whirlwind of activity. Police and crime lab techs traipsed in and out of the house for what seemed like eternity. Julia was exhausted. For the first couple of hours she had stood outside the large house waiting for the police to tell her it was okay to go in, and finally she simply tried to walk in the door.

"I'm sorry ma'am," she was told.

She nodded and wiped her nose. She knew. Right from

the gut, she knew that Mae was not coming back. Seth simply leaned up on his car, texting and playing games on his state of the art iPhone. She walked over to him.

"Aren't you even worried?" Her hands were on her hips.

"Well sure, Julia." But his eyes never left the screen.

His attitude made her angry. She turned and grabbed the front of his shirt and pulled him in close.

"How can you be so cold?" she demanded.

He stared at her for a moment. "Look, I know you guys are unnaturally close, but really, we don't have any reason to get upset yet, do we? I mean, for all we know, she could be shacked up somewhere with a guy."

Rage built inside her and every ounce of her wanted to knock his snotty little block off. How did he not know how wonderful his stepmother was?

SETH BIT HIS THUMBNAIL thoughtfully. Why hadn't those goons called yet? They were supposed to call by morning and demand a healthy ransom. Then Seth could've called the police playing the concerned stepson. But no, Julia had to butt her big nose into it. How had she known? Now, he looked like a heel or worse, part of the plan. He could still pull it off, he decided.

In a day or two Mae would be back, but things would be different. They would've made her sign over the trust to him.

It served her right after refusing him access to what was his. After all, the Arbeson fortune wasn't hers to control. Arbeson blood didn't run in her veins. It was her fault he owed so much to those thugs. If he had the control he deserved, he wouldn't have had to borrow. What had his father been thinking to make her trustee? His anger bubbled to the surface again. Who did she think she was to deprive him? They said they wouldn't hurt her much, just enough to be convincing. She'd be home nagging him soon enough.

CHAPTER SEVEN

DETECTIVE SERGEANT TONY LANGE SWALLOWED HARD. Never before had a woman sent his heart racing the first moment he saw her. She was beautiful. Her long golden blonde hair was streaked with strands of silver that illuminated her freckled face. Tears clung in her soft blue eyes. She stood steadfastly as the officers searched for any clues to her friend's whereabouts.

How could he tell her that there was little, if anything, to go on? No fingerprints, very little trace — all of which appeared to belong to the victim — nothing to help find Mae Arbeson or convict her abductors.

Tony sighed. He believed Julia's concern was warranted. And then there was the kid. The smug little shit surely had something to do with Mrs. Arbeson's disappearance. Tony's guess was that he had conspired to kidnap or maybe even murder his stepmother. The Arbesons had a lot of money. More than a nineteen-year old would know what to do with.

The woman dabbed at her eyes again and hugged herself as she leaned up against her SUV. Tony's heart melted. He shoved his fists into his jeans and walked over to her. "Ms. Metcalf?"

Her expression said it all. That it was about damn time someone came to talk to her. She watched him as he approached.

"Ah look," he said, running a hand over his weathered face. "We didn't find any blood, or any signs of forced entry. The alarm was shut off manually. There's not much that would prove abduction. For all we can tell, she might've just had a tantrum, like the kid said."

She dropped her arms to her sides. "You expect me to believe that? Did you talk to Seth?"

"Yes. He has an alibi, and I confirmed it with his credit card company. He was at the Wherehouse." He raised his palms.

"What about the security cameras?" She asked.

"Not working. He says there is an appointment with the alarm company to fix it tomorrow."

"That's damned convenient. What about the guards?"

"No one used the front gate."

"Service entrance?" Her arms crossed over her chest.

"The guard was making his rounds, and the gate doesn't appear to be tampered with." He looked into her eyes.

"Huh." Her cheeks flushed and her jaw tensed.

"I'm sorry, but until or unless we have some evidence that gives us anything further, we're done here." He fervently wished he could reach out and smooth the crease in her forehead. He frowned. *What the hell was that?* He didn't need another heartache in his life.

"That's it?" Julia asked. "You just leave as if nothing ever happened? Don't you suppose she'd be home by now if she was off on a lark?"

He kept looking into her eyes. He felt like he was looking at her soul, and he liked what he saw. "We'll make a report. I'll give Mr. Arbeson a copy. You can have one too, if you like. But I'm afraid we've spent as much time here as we're able."

"Can I go back in?" Seth asked. "I'm getting hungry."

Tony turned to him. "Sure. We'll be out of the way shortly."

He watched as the young man sauntered back into the house before turning his attention back to Julia. "Hey," he said tenderly. "I know she's your friend. I have her picture and the report. I'll keep my ear to the ground on this, okay?"

Julia looked into his eyes. He hoped she saw his sincerity.

"If you don't believe anything is amiss, why would you do that?" Her voice was tight with anger and frustration.

A slight smile crept across his face. "I didn't say I didn't believe you." He led her away from the house a bit. "Don't take this wrong, but do you think the kid might have had anything to do with it?"

She stopped. Her brow wrinkled for a moment. Clearly, the idea hit her hard. "Possibly. He's done a lot of bad things, but nothing like this."

"We won't talk anymore here. Don't look," he said, his eyes never leaving hers. "But he's watching from the window. Take my card and call me. I'll be at the precinct after 7:00. We'll talk." He handed it to her and walked away.

EXHAUSTED, JULIA WENT HOME. Her mind was filled with Mae and Detective Tony Lange. She pictured him briefly. He was well over six feet with a head full of rakish salt and pepper hair. The color matched his slightly unkempt mustache. His deep brown eyes were flecked with bits of gold and sparkled in the light. But those thoughts were for another time.

She crawled into her bed. Her heart was aching, and

although she had succeeded in fending off the dread until now, her defenses finally collapsed. She wailed and prayed and begged and cried nearly all day. As twilight approached, she finally fell into a fitful sleep.

CLOUDS. HUNDREDS OF THEM, swirling and melding. She batted at them in the hope that she could see beyond them, but each time she swatted one away, another was behind it. The one she was sitting upon moved slowly. She shifted from side to side impatiently. At last, she just sat and waited while the cloud took her to her destination.

Mae sat on another cloud, eyes closed. She looked to be in deep meditation.

"Mae, it's me," Julia cried. She reached out to her friend as the two clouds passed, but couldn't quite reach. The cloud tipped over. Julia toppled off and began to free fall.

She awoke just as the sun began to color the sky. Her hand flew as she scribbled the fragmented bits of the dream. She desperately tried to remember them all. Chamomile tea did little to soothe her raw nerves so she padded barefoot out to the backyard to tend her flowers and the lush trumpet vine that climbed up the back of the house. She buried her face in the blooms and inhaled their subtle fragrance.

The original vine had been planted by her grandfather. She and her beloved "Papa" would carefully prune, nip buds, water, and tie slender branches together. When Julia bought the house after divorcing Jeff, Papa planted a cutting from his, and told her that a part of him would always be in her yard, right there with her. He passed away shortly thereafter.

She cared for the vine as vigilantly as they had tended the parent plant. Her hand grazed the glossy leaves and delicate orange blossoms. With the motion, she connected with her grandfather. It soothed her aching heart.

She slowly moved into the kitchen and made more tea. As she did, she picked up the detective's card and stared at it for a long time. A sigh escaped her lips as she dialed and closed her eyes.

"Lange," he said.

"Detective, this is Julia Metcalf calling. I met you at Mae Arbeson's yesterday?" She pinched the bridge of her nose as though it would stop the gnawing fear in her stomach.

"Yes, Ms. Metcalf," he replied.

Did she hear a smile in his voice? "I'd like to talk to you about Mae. When can we meet?"

"Have you had breakfast?" His voice was deep and comforting, with just a hint of the south.

Her stomach growled at the mere mention. "No."

"Great. Can you meet me at Ma's Diner in, say twenty minutes?"

Ma's had always struck her as a greasy little place. Her nose wrinkled. Her sensible side thought about an alternative nutrition source.

"Sure," Julia said, quickly calculating how long she would have to make herself presentable and still get to Ma's.

TONY WAITED PATIENTLY IN the worn vinyl booth; his long legs stretched out into the aisle. He sat in the last booth for just that reason, but still was careful to move them as the waitresses hustled to and from the kitchen. The place hadn't been painted since Tony was a boy, and the decades old booths seemed the newest things in the place, but Ma made the best eggs in town.

Julia was running late. In all fairness, he hadn't given her much time. When she appeared at the door, she looked just as beautiful as he remembered. Her hair hung in a braid over her left shoulder, and her arm was wrapped around a brightly colored notebook. He stood when she approached then took her jacket and hung it on the hook next to the booth.

"Did you get any rest?" Tony asked. Worry shadowed his face.

"Yes, some."

"Please, sit. Coffee?"

"Yes, thanks."

He nodded to the waitress and turned his full attention back to Julia. "As I told you earlier, I believe you. Something's happened to Mrs. Arbeson. My gut feel is that her stepson knows more than he's saying. The problem is that there's no evidence."

Tears threatened to spill over as Julia answered. "I know something terrible has happened."

The waitress plopped two ceramic mugs onto the scarred table and filled them, displaying astounding speed and accuracy.

"What'll ya have?" she asked with a hand on her hip. It was part of the Ma's Diner experience.

"Have you been here before?" Tony asked Julia.

"No." She couldn't contain the nose wrinkle.

"Then please, allow me." He turned to the scowling waitress and displayed a most disarming smile.

The waitress rolled her eyes. "How about today, pal?"

"Number three, rise and shine, slinger with a pig. For both of us." He smiled at Julia.

The waitress sneered and said, "Right," before sauntering away. He watched her turn toward the kitchen and yell his order word for word.

Julia smiled a little. "What did you order?"

"Eggs, sunny side up, hash, and bacon." His brown eyes twinkled. "Tell me, Ms. Metcalf, how long have you known

Mrs. Arbeson?"

"Please, call me Julia. I've known her since we were eight." She knuckled back a tear.

"Did the kid call you?"

"No. He hadn't even noticed she was gone."

"Then how did you know?"

She looked around the diner, but didn't really see it. "I just knew, and I called to see if she was okay. That's when Seth found out. I made him go look for her."

"I don't understand. How did you know to call her?"

She sighed and looked into his eyes. They were surrounded by laugh lines that etched his face, but he didn't look old at all — just that he'd spent a lot of time outdoors. He was handsome in a rugged sort of way.

"You probably wouldn't believe me." She lowered her eyes.

"Try me."

"Okay." She took a deep breath. "I have dreams sometimes."

"You mean precognitive dreams? Wow!" he remarked.

Her eyes narrowed. She couldn't tell if he was serious or being sarcastic. "I'm not sure precognitive is the right term. Sometimes they're psychic, sometimes precognitive."

The waitress unceremoniously dropped their plates in front of them. "Two number threes for the smart ass." She refilled their coffee and walked away.

"The service here..." Julia began.

"It's all about the food, not the ambience, although it is... unique," he replied. "Try your eggs."

Cautiously, she scooped up a small forkful and tasted. "Wow, these are really good!"

"The best," he said as he attacked his plate. "So, did you see her kidnapping in your dream?"

"No. It's almost never that easy. I dreamt that she turned

into a firefly and said she didn't want to go. I know that sounds kind of benign, but believe me, it wasn't."

"Huh. I don't suppose her captors were spiders?"

She dropped her fork. Fire blazed in her eyes.

His heart lurched, and he couldn't swallow.

"Look, I shouldn't have even told you. Thanks for breakfast." Her oval face was red, and twin creases appeared between her eyebrows. She grabbed for her purse when he caught her hand.

"Wait. I didn't mean it the way it sounded. I guess I was just hoping for a lead, and it seemed to follow. I'm sorry."

Her anger subsided, and she sat back down. "Look, if it'll help find Mae, I'll tell you the whole dream, or you can read it for yourself."

"Read it?"

"Yeah, I write the dreams down. The details fade fast, and I don't want them lost."

"When did you start writing them down?"

"I was about fourteen. It was after Mae's brother went for a midnight swim in their pool. He apparently dove in on the shallow end and broke his neck, and drowned. I dreamed it, and the next day when her parents asked me how I knew, I couldn't answer. I still don't know exactly what I dreamt."

"I find that very intriguing."

"You don't know the half of it."

Julia handed Tony the journal containing the dream about Mae.

CHAPTER EIGHT

LATER THAT MORNING, SHE CALLED SETH. She dialed several times before he deigned to answer.

"Any word yet?" Her tone was less than happy.

"Julia, I'm sure everything is fine. Stop worrying."

"You haven't answered my question, Seth."

"No. No word yet. I'll call you. I promise."

Yeah, I'll hold my breath for your call, Julia thought as she disconnected. She bit her thumbnail and spent the rest of the day calling everyone that she and Mae knew.

MAE WAS DRESSED IN *a beautiful gossamer gown. She was smiling, with her arms outstretched holding a trinket box in her hands. It was gilded and in the shape of a large egg.*

"Take it, Jule," Mae said. "I don't need it anymore."

"No. I want you. I don't care about any stupid egg."

"It's very valuable, and I want you to have it," Mae entreated. *"Please. It's a part of me you can keep forever."*

"No Mae. I want you. Don't leave me."

"I'll never leave you, Jule. I'll always be with you."

"What is this egg?"

"Don't let it go. Even if it seems more trouble than it's worth. Hold tight. Don't let them take it."

Julia awoke and pondered the dream as she recorded it in her journal. Even the minute details of Mae's dress were included. She recalled each shimmering bead. Lost in her reverie, the ringing phone startled her. She trembled slightly as she reached for it.

"Julia? It's Tony."

Her face relaxed, and she found herself smiling. "Hi, I forgot to thank you for breakfast yesterday morning."

"It was my pleasure. The service was so memorable, I might just ask you again."

Julia laughed. "Have you found anything?"

"Not yet, but I am keeping an eye open. I thought I would tell you that I'm digging into Seth a little. That kid stands to inherit a fortune."

"Yeah, I know."

"I checked his record. He hasn't gotten into any real trouble."

"You forget who his father was, Tony. He was, and is, plenty of trouble. His father bought his way out more than once."

"Okay, I'll check a little further. In the meantime, can you can get into Mae's house and have a look around for anything unusual or out of place? I could use your insight, since you're so familiar with the scene."

"I can do that," she replied.

Thirty minutes later, she was standing outside Mae's house pounding on the door. Elsa answered. Tears clung in her eyes. "Oh, Miss Julia! Have they found her yet?"

"No, I haven't heard anything. Have you cleaned up her room yet?"

Elsa took a moment to stop wringing her hands and shut the massive door. "No, I didn't know if I should."

"I'm glad, because I'd like to do it. I need to do it. Is that okay?"

"Mr. Seth won't like it." A look of concern tensed Elsa's face and she lowered her voice, glancing quickly around. "He thinks the "little people" should perform such menial tasks."

Julia smiled and patted Elsa's shoulder. "I'll tell him I horned in on you. Why don't we do it together? It'll look better."

Elsa nodded vigorously. "I'll get us a tray of coffee."

CHAPTER NINE

TONY WRESTLED WITH HIS FEELINGS FOR Julia. Her glowing hair reminded him of a rippling sheet of honey-colored silk and her eyes were the same hue as forget-me-nots on a clear spring morning. Looking into them turned his insides to mush. He shook off the image. He refused to fall in love again. The pain inflicted by his ex-wife left his heart scarred, even though it had been more than a decade. He wasn't about to let that kind of hurt happen again.

Wendy was his high school sweetheart. They had married in 1994, just a year after graduation. Eight years later, he walked in on her and her lover in the middle of the afternoon.

"Tony!" She gathered the blankets and sheets around herself. Her thick brown hair splayed over her face. Her make-up was smudged and her cheeks feverishly flushed.

His gaze fell upon her partner. He looked like a weasel.

"She, uh, she didn't tell me she was married." He quickly grabbed his jeans.

"Oh you liar." She narrowed her eyes at her lover.

"He's got a gun, Wendy."

"Get the fuck out of here before I use it." Tony's hands were balled up into fists. His eyes were on fire.

Silence hung like a thick bank of storm clouds until Weasel made his hasty exit, yanking his shirt and jacket on as he hopped out the door, pants at half-mast. When Tony heard the front door slam, he turned to Wendy. She pulled on her robe.

"Why?" His face twisted into the mass of hurt and confusion.

"Why? What do you mean, why?" She pulled the robe tighter around her. "You're never here. It's always the job."

"Darlin,' that's just not true."

"Not true?" Her voice rose to a shrill scream. "What about my birthday? Or our anniversary?"

"I took you to L'Orange for dinner."

"And left me at the table. Alone."

He bent his head and shoved his hands into his pockets. "You're right. But we promised each other we'd be true."

Tears rolled down her face and her jaw set. "I'm supposed to be the most important thing in your life. The Job is your mistress. She's been your priority since you graduated from the academy. I've always taken a back seat. You've left me in the middle of parties, family functions, and Christmas. You've left when I needed you most. Whenever I was sick, when my mother was in the hospital, you weren't there for me. Nothing is sacred. I don't see how anyone could expect a cop's wife to be faithful."

"Why didn't you tell me sooner?"

"Why didn't you notice? Why didn't you keep *your* promises?"

He sagged and sat on the bed defeated. "You're right."

Wendy dropped the robe and pulled on a pair of sweats and a tee shirt. She yanked a suitcase from her closet and began throwing her clothes in it.

"What are you doing?"

"I'm leaving. Then you can spend all your time with your job and that asshole, Dale."

"Wait. Aren't we even going to discuss this?"

"No."

"I don't even get a chance to change the things I can?"

"No. It's too late."

"I'll take a job doing private security."

"Don't bother."

"I'll do whatever it takes, Wendy. Please don't do this."

"I can't stay here now."

"So that's it?"

"I guess so."

After a week of calling in sick, Dale came to Tony's house looking for him. The constant rapping pounded Tony's aching head mercilessly. Finally, he opened the door and squinted at Dale blearily. "What?" he slurred.

Dale looked him over and whistled. "Personally, I don't think Wendy was worth all this." He pushed past Tony into the living room. "Jesus, kid. You stink. Take a shower. Then we're gonna clean up this dump. You could sponsor a 'how many beer cans in this picture?' contest."

"She left me."

Dale's face softened. "Yeah, I figured that out for myself."

"You know what really bugs me?"

"What?"

Tony ran a hand over the week's worth of stubble on his face. "I never knew."

"That's usually how it goes."

"Dale, I had no idea. Some detective, huh?"

Dale's mouth curled upward and he clapped Tony's shoulder. "Chalk it up to training, kid. Get your stinky ass in the shower."

CHAPTER TEN

As she climbed the grand staircase, Julia paused now and then to touch things and fill her mind with Mae. When she reached the master suite, she hesitated outside the door. Slowly, she turned the knob. The room still looked as it did before the police searched the suite.

With a heavy sigh, Julia picked up the bedding from the floor. Absently, she refolded Mae's duvet, and placed it gently on the cedar chest at the foot of the antique bed. For a while, she just wandered the room, looking at the things that meant so much to Mae. She felt something crunch under her foot. It was a picture frame. Julia picked it up. Shards of glass fell like jagged snowflakes onto the polished wood floor.

Elsa knocked and entered laden with a silver tray. She set it on the dressing table and poured coffee into Julia's favorite china cup. Mae had found it on one of their antique shopping excursions. It was delicate and painted with tiny butterflies and flowers. She'd called it 'Jule's happy cup.' Julia smiled at the memory and sipped her coffee.

Elsa swept up the glass shards, and Julia renewed her resolve. She focused once again on the picture that now occupied a bent, glassless frame. She turned it over, and began to cry. Elsa rushed over to put an arm around her. Two carefree joyful faces glowed from the photo — Julia and Mae the summer after seventh grade. They'd been swimming.

Julia started to laugh through her tears. "We look like a couple of drowned rats," she said, wiping her tears on her sleeve.

Elsa handed her a tissue. "I can take care of this, Miss Julia."

"No, thanks. I've got to do it." She stood up and took a deep breath. With a nod, she began to pick up the strewn items and put them in their proper place. Once the room was tidied and cleaned, Julia and Elsa sat side by side on the satin chaise and looked around the room.

Julia noticed it first. She bent over at the edge of the bed and carefully lifted the small tuft of hair. There was a bit of flesh on the end, as though it had been pulled out viciously. It was dark, like Mae's.

"Oh," Julia sobbed. "Elsa, I need a plastic bag. The kind with the zipper, if you can find one." Tears coursed down both of their faces as Elsa hurried to the kitchen.

Julia placed the dark strands in the bag and zippered it closed. For a moment, she stared at the hair. She wasn't sure, but she didn't think it was Mae's. She clicked open her cell and dialed Tony's number with shaking hands.

"Lange."

"Tony?" Julia sobbed.

"Julia, what's wrong?"

"I found something in Mae's room."

"What did you find?"

"We were making the bed and I found a tuft of hair," she

sniffed. "It looks like Mae's hair color, but I'm not sure. There's a chunk of skin attached to it."

"Okay, just stop and take a breath. What did you do with it?"

"I put it in a zipper bag."

"Okay. Why don't I take you to lunch, and you can give it to me?"

Julia glanced in the mirror. Her hair looked unkempt and her mascara ran from her puffy red eyes. "Um, okay. I'll need a few minutes to pull myself together, though."

"Sure. How about I pick you up at noon?"

"That sounds good. Do you want my address?"

"I'm a cop, Julia. I'll find it."

"Is it that easy?"

Tony chuckled. "In all the excitement, you must have forgotten that you gave that information for the police report."

CHAPTER ELEVEN

TONY PULLED UP IN A CANDY apple red 1969 GTO convertible.

"Wow! This is a great car," Julia said, looking at it like it was edible.

He smiled. "Want the top down?"

"Oh, yes." Julia slid into the front seat and ran an admiring hand along the dash. "Where'd you get such a beauty?"

"She was my dad's," he said as he worked the latches and carefully folded the top down. "He and I restored her on weekends. That was only because we couldn't afford all the pieces we needed at once. It was a chrome strip here and a knob there until we found all of 'em. Or at least enough to get her on the road." He smiled proudly.

"Well, I'll get the bag with the hair out of my purse."

"No, wait 'til we stop. The wind might take it."

"I hadn't thought of that." Julia tried to hold her long blonde hair back out of her face, but it flew everywhere.

They pulled up to a gorgeous lakefront, with a beach and

a park nearby. The trees swayed slowly in the breeze, and the lake had a fresh clean smell. The waves made soothing lapping sounds as they kissed the shore.

"I don't see any restaurants," she commented.

He simply smiled and opened the trunk. Inside was a blanket and picnic basket roughly the same vintage as the car. He handed the blanket to Julia and said, "Pick a spot."

"Detective Lange, do you often take witnesses on picnics?" she asked, smiling as they walked to a quiet, shady spot.

"No, but technically, we don't have a crime yet, so I figure we're safe. Besides," he said looking into her eyes, "I find myself very attracted to you." He took her hand.

Smiling shyly, she spread the blanket under a huge tree. Tony unpacked the deli sandwiches, along with potato salad and soda.

A pleasant shiver travelled through Julia's body when Tony smiled at her. He was propped up on one elbow, with his long legs crossed at the top of his silver-tipped cowboy boots. The crinkles at the corners of his eyes were particularly attractive. He ran a hand through his tousled salt and pepper hair. Her mother would have called them piano player's hands with their long bones. She'd have noticed how handsome he was, too. Julia listened as he made small talk. Not so much hearing what he said as the way he said it.

His deep, slightly raspy voice resonated comfortably as he began telling her a story about his boyhood dog, Buster. She was suddenly overcome with the desire to kiss him. Her cheeks grew hot.

"Are you blushing?"

Her hands flew to her face as the redness spread and deepened. "Um, I just got kinda hot, that's all."

He chuckled. "Tell me what you were thinking."

She shook her head. "Please, go on with your story.

Buster, wasn't it?"

He grinned at her for a moment. "Okay. So Buster ran off with my brand new wallet, containing my fishing license. There I stood, my first brush with the law, and I was unable to provide proof of my innocence."

"You were a juvenile delinquent then?"

He roared with laughter and pushed to his feet. She took his hand as he helped her up. "I hate to cut this short," he said, "but I've got to get back to work." He held both her hands. "I'd like to take you to dinner some time."

She smiled. "I'd like that."

She tied her hair back and slid into the GTO. He got behind the wheel, and they started back to Julia's when his phone rang.

"Lange." He listened for a moment. "On my way."

He glanced over at Julia. She smiled and tried to smooth the strands that had escaped the elastic and whipped chaotically around her face.

He pulled up in front of her house. Something in his eyes seemed off.

"Is everything okay, Tony?"

"I hope so." He walked her to the door. "Can I kiss you?"

She smiled. "I'd like that." He kissed her lightly then turned to leave.

"Wait! The baggie," she said, digging into her tote bag.

"Thanks."

CHAPTER TWELVE

TONY'S STOMACH FELT LIKE THE OCTOPUS ride at the county fair. He hated going to the morgue, especially right after lunch. He braced himself and pushed open the swinging door into the autopsy suite. The smell of chemicals and death pummeled his innards.

"God, Harry. How can you eat in here?" Tony asked. He nearly retched.

Dr. Harrington Welsh turned from the counter sporting a mouthful of peanut butter and jelly sandwich. "You get used to it after a while, my friend."

He smiled and set down his lunch. Gesturing toward the table, he donned a pair of rubber gloves and handed a set to Tony.

Mae's waxen face and body were mottled with bruises. Her face was unrecognizable. "Have you ID'd her?" Tony asked.

"Not officially. Somebody really did a number on her. Look at these contusions." Harry lifted her head gently and turned it slightly.

"Wow. What did they use?"

"Looks like a sap. With some strength behind it, I might add. I also found some marks that were caused by a considerably sized fist and maybe a boot or two."

Tony whistled. "Who still uses a sap? I thought they went out with prohibition."

Harry nodded.

"Same basic physical description as the Arbeson woman."

"And her watch was engraved." He gestured toward the bag of personal effects. "It's very likely her, but with her shattered jaw and missing teeth, I can't use her dental records for an official positive ID now. We'll have to wait for DNA. I've put a rush on it."

Tony nodded. "Cause?"

"I'm putting cause of death as 'shit beaten out of her.'"

"Correct me if I'm wrong," Tony began.

"With pleasure," Harry replied.

"With all of this bruising, it looks like she fought them for a while under considerable duress."

"You're right. I'd venture an educated guess at several hours, minimally. Seven ribs broken, cheekbone fractured, shattered jaw, internal hemorrhaging. Defensive wounds that broke one wrist and did extensive soft tissue damage to the other. She suffered greatly." Harry laid a hand on her shoulder. "Poor woman."

Tony sighed at the thought of having to tell Julia.

"The good news is that her knuckles are bruised and one foot has a couple of broken phalanges. She got in a couple of decent licks."

"Anything under her nails?"

"I'm glad you asked." Harry smiled again. "Our brave girl scratched her assailant hard enough to draw blood. The samples contained flecks consistent with male facial hair, so with any luck, our perp is sporting a bodacious triple gash on his face."

"Harry, nobody says *perp* anymore. You gotta stop watching those old cop shows on TV."

Harry merely smiled. "I've bagged and tagged her clothing. There's a miniscule amount of trace, but there's a lot of dirt and sand. With the rain we've had, I don't expect much."

"Well, here's a hair sample. It's tainted, but get what you can from it."

"Where'd you get this?"

"Julia Metcalf. She found it at the Arbeson estate. In the bedroom. Bagged it herself."

"Shit."

"Can't put the toothpaste back in the tube, Harry."

"Yeah. I'll run it through, but we won't be able to use it in the report."

Tony nodded and stood staring at Mae silently for several minutes.

"Tony," Harry remarked. "I've known you a lot of years. I know you despise coming in here. But you do it with every victim, every time. And you stand there and stare at them for a while. Sometimes you even touch them, the entire time looking like you're going to pass out. If you are so disturbed, why not just go on the report? Everything will be in there. You wouldn't be the only one."

Tony's gaze never wavered from Mae. "I stare at them because I don't want to forget what the murderers did to them. I don't want to ever be so removed from a victim that I don't turn over every stone, every time. Most of them didn't deserve what they got, but they do deserve to have their killers brought to justice. Otherwise I couldn't live with myself."

"Wow, it's true. Melhus is your mother."

Tony laughed at the thought of his old partner, Dale.

"Yeah, I guess he is at that. Thanks, Harry. Let me know when you know."

"Will do. Poker. Thursday night. My place. Bring your own booze this time."

"You're on."

CHAPTER THIRTEEN

JULIA STARED AT HER SCULPTURE HOPING some inspiration would jump out at her. She usually enjoyed creating art from useless parts of old cars, trucks, boats, bicycles, and machines. She chose the parts that spoke to her. Then she would methodically clean, drill, paint, and position until they were transformed into art. She favored using rich color and wrought iron. Most of her works moved using solar or wind energy.

One of her pieces stood proudly in front of the local art museum. It boasted louvered fins to catch the wind and set it in motion. Mae swore that she had not influenced the board, but Julia suspected it was so.

The thought of Mae made her stomach lurch. A faint glimmer of hope ran through her, but soon the dread returned.

Tears welled up. She brushed at them, tipped down her welding helmet, and tried to lose herself in her creation.

After a few more minutes, she gave up. The anger built inside her until an uncontrolled growl gurgled out. She threw her welding gloves across the room and fisted her hands at her hips. She paced a few minutes, hoping to walk off the tension. With a sigh, she hung up her helmet and leather apron. Faintly, she heard the doorbell ring and she headed to answer the door.

Tony's face said it all. Tears welled up and spilled over. He wrapped his arms around her and pulled her close.

"I'm so sorry, Jule."

She buried her face in his shoulder and sobbed, "No, no, no."

Her breathing heaved and shuddered. He stroked her head and kissed her brow, and just let her cry. The warmth of his arms soothed her.

Gently, he whispered to her. "It's okay. I'm here. I'll stay right here."

It was some time before she quieted. As the racking sobs diminished, she looked at his face. "Oh Tony," she said, wiping her face, and backing away. "I'm sorry."

"It's okay." He took her hand and looked into her eyes, smiling slightly. "I've got broad shoulders and you're welcome to cry on them anytime."

She studied his face for a moment. "Thanks. You're good with hysterics." She grabbed a tissue, and then noticed the condition of his shirt. "Oh, look at the mess I've made!" she cried, touching his shirt. The tears poured over again.

"It's okay. Shh," he whispered and drew her in again.

At last, she pulled herself together. Wiping her flushed nose again, she pulled gently away. "I'll make some coffee, and you can give me the details."

At that moment, she straightened her spine, gathered her strength, and prepared herself to hear the worst.

CHAPTER FOURTEEN

TONY FOLLOWED HER TO THE KITCHEN and leaned in the doorway, crossing one foot over the other. He couldn't pinpoint what made it so interesting to watch her scoop coffee grounds into the small coffee maker on her counter. He had already decided not to tell her everything. She was too vulnerable.

"Sit down," she said quietly as she set the coffee on the small dinette.

"Thanks."

She let out a long sigh. "Okay, tell me."

He took her hand. "We found her. I'm so sorry, Jule. I know how close you were."

"Where?"

"In the woods north of town," he replied. "She was found by a hunter. It was a shallow grave."

What he didn't tell her was how she had died. It ran a shudder through him even to think of it. The killer or killers — it appeared there may have been more than one — had been brutal. Julia didn't need that piece of information.

"Can I see her?"

Tony fidgeted. "Jule, she passed away that first night. It's better if you remember her the way she was."

Every fiber of his being wanted to protect her from the truth.

She looked into his eyes. "Has Seth been notified?"

"Yes, I had to notify him first, since he's her next of kin."

"Did he seem shocked, or sad?"

"I watched his reaction pretty carefully. I don't know if he was involved or not. It's possible, I think."

Again, Tony kept part of the truth from her. He was, in fact, certain of Seth's involvement. It was Tony's opinion that Seth had faked his shocked expression when told of Mae's death. Tony purposely gave him the graphic details in order to see his reaction. He blanched and appeared sickened by the description. The kid very well might have contracted for her kidnapping or even death, but hadn't expected the means.

"All right. What sort of clues did you uncover to find her murderer?"

"Some trace evidence which is being run through forensics as we speak. We suspect there was more than one person."

"Poor Mae!"

Suddenly, Julia looked at Tony. Her hand flew to her mouth. She was afraid to ask. "She wasn't... you know?"

He rubbed her arms. "There's no evidence of that." It was the only way it could have been worse.

Julia nodded. She met his gaze and stared for just a moment.

"Well, I'm sure there are things you need to do, and I'm going to curl up and have another cry."

"I can stay if you need me to," he said, tenderly taking her hand.

"Thanks, but I think I need some alone time."

"I'll call you later."

He got up, and she walked him to the door. As he reached for the knob, she laid a hand on his shoulder. He turned to her. She reached up and kissed his cheek. It was a lingering kiss that sent energy shooting through him like fireworks. It took every ounce of self-control he had not to gather her up and start something that could end awkwardly.

"Thanks, Tony," she whispered as he stepped out the door.

CHAPTER FIFTEEN

JULIA CRIED HERSELF TO SLEEP. WHEN she awoke, she called Seth.

"Yeah?" he answered groggily.

"Seth, are you okay?" she asked.

"My stepmother is dead. Do you think I'm okay?" There was no emotion in his voice.

"No, I'm sure it's been very difficult. Do you want me to take care of the funeral arrangements?"

"Julia, we have people to do those things. You've never really gotten our lifestyle, have you?"

"I'm just trying to help, Seth. You'll let me know if I can do anything, won't you?"

"Yeah." With that, he disconnected.

The funeral was scheduled for two days later. Tony escorted Julia to the funeral home. No expense had been spared, and Mae's mahogany coffin was covered in a flower spray bigger than Julia had ever seen. She cringed a little at how puny her flowers looked next to the gigantic arrangements sent by the very rich and famous. She approached the coffin and dropped down onto the kneeler set before it.

"Mae?" she prayed. "Oh, Mae. You can't know how much I'll miss you. I feel so empty." Her fingertips touched the glossy wood.

Julia had never considered the possibility that Mae wouldn't always be in her life. Suddenly, a wave of sadness threatened to drown her. All the little things about Mae that she had taken for granted flashed before her. Her musical voice and the tiny lines that just started to appear at the corners of her soft brown eyes; the way Julia drove her to laugh until she snorted, much to the horror of her socially elite husband; and the way her halo of thick brown curls bounced merrily at her every movement. Even as children, Julia knew that she was the only person with whom Mae could just be Mae.

She stared at the coffin and dabbed at the tear that trickled down her face. Whose advice would she ask now? Who would counsel her on men and commiserate at their platitudes and boyish behaviors? Who would render a wholeheartedly honest opinion on clothes, shoes, and hair colors? With whom could she gossip and giggle like a young girl? Mae knew her inside and out, and still loved her. How would she live without her friend, conspirator, and sister of the heart?

She shook her head and blinked back the tears with superhuman will power.

After the service, Julia approached Seth and hugged him. He stood stiffly as though he couldn't wait for it to be over.

"Mae would have been proud of you today, Seth. You've conducted yourself very well."

"Yeah, well she's not here, is she?" he retorted.

"I believe she is." Julia turned and walked away. *What a*

little jerk.

Tony dropped her off at home. She waved until he was out of sight, and the smile faded from her face. A sigh shuddered out as she unlocked the door and gathered her mail. The envelope from Halberg, Finch, Lazlo, and Drew caught her attention.

The letter inside stated there was to be a meeting at the estate about Mae's last wishes.

She dropped the letter and the rest of the mail on the kitchen table and kicked off her heels. Slowly, she climbed the stairs. The storm of emotion she shook off at the service doubled in strength. As she entered her room, the tears started. She couldn't have stopped them any more than anyone could stop the tides. Wrapping her favorite cotton quilt around her, she curled up on her bed in a tight ball and let it all out until she fell into a fitful sleep.

"Jule," Mae said. "Don't you want to play dolls anymore?"

"It's not that. I don't want him to play." Julia pointed to the Sasquatch who sat on the floor between the two young girls. In her trembling hand, Julia held a doll that looked very much like her.

"I know, but he has to play."

"Says who?"

"Says him, and I'm scared of him." Mae's voice shook.

The Sasquatch grunted and flipped the Julia doll into the air. The doll landed headfirst on the hardwood floor a few feet away. The Sasquatch roared, showing its sharp teeth. Slowly, it stood to its full height, striking its hairy head on the ceiling. It bellowed again and grabbed Mae by the throat. He shook her violently and her body went limp. He tossed her aside like an unwanted toy and turned to Julia, hairy arms outstretched.

She awoke sweating and breathing heavily. Her heart rate soared. She gathered up her journal and pen, and wrote frantically. Her hands shook badly enough that she had to scribble out several words and rewrite them. Once the dream was written down, she felt calmer, but still couldn't sleep. It seemed that there was some message in it, but Julia felt confused.

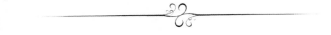

SHE COULDN'T IMAGINE WHAT she had to do with Mae's estate, but she made it a point to be on time to the meeting. Perhaps Mae had left her a little something to remember her by.

Seth and four attorneys flanked the long table in the conference room at the Arbeson estate. Elsa stood steadfastly at the door. Julia couldn't fathom why she needed to be present. Surely the mail would suffice for whatever small remembrance that Mae left her.

One of the attorneys approached her. "Ms. Metcalf, I presume?"

Julia nodded. "I'm Phineas Halberg. Just call me Phin, everyone does." He took her hand in both of his. "I'm very sorry for your loss."

Julia shook hands with the tall, slender man. His clever eyes were set squarely between his thinning hair and hawkish nose.

Once everyone was seated, Phin began. "First of all, we'd like to express our deepest condolences. Mrs. Arbeson was an extraordinary person."

You have no idea, Julia thought.

"We are here to read Mrs. Arbeson's will. I would ask your indulgence that we may do so uninterrupted, and save your questions for after the reading. Is that clear?"

"Yes," everyone murmured.

"Good. Then we shall begin." He read all of the legalese and then started in with the disposal of the estate. "First, to Elsa, my companion and faithful friend, I leave the sum of one million dollars, and my 1955 Thunderbird. Enjoy it, Elsa."

Elsa was dumbfounded. She grabbed the closest chair and sat down hard. Her mouth dropped open and she stared into space. Julia rushed over to pat her back and ask if she was all right. She nodded and Julia reluctantly sat back down.

"To Seth I leave only the house. Your Arbeson trust will be distributed on schedule for the remainder of your life, if necessary. You have not proven that you can be responsible with the funds unless they are meted out as they have been. Learn to live within your means, and in five years, the executor will meet with the attorneys to reconsider handing the trust over to you."

Seth's face turned bright crimson. He opened his mouth to speak.

"Seth, please wait until we are finished to comment," Phineas Halberg interjected.

He turned back to the probate documents and continued. "Next, to my dearest and closest friend, Julia Metcalf, I leave all of my remaining worldly possessions and all of my holdings except the manse. I realize this is a huge responsibility, Jule. I know you will do what is best. For this reason, I am naming you trustee for The Arbeson Trust."

Seth stood up and screamed, "This is an outrage! I will not allow it!"

The lawyers looked at each other. Seth pointed an accusing finger at Julia. "You have no idea what it takes to be an Arbeson. My trust is none of your business. It's mine!" He turned to the lawyers. "You *will* fix this."

"I'm sorry, young man. These are your stepmother's wishes. It's all quite legal."

Seth leaned across the table and into Julia's personal space. "You'll administer the trust as I say. Do you hear me Julia? I'm warning you."

Julia sat calmly. It was just another of Seth's tantrums.

"Your stepmother has made this decision to help you grow up, Seth. You've just proven you haven't."

"Son of a bitch!" He shoved his way out of the room and slammed the door.

All eyes were on the closed door for a moment, and then the lawyer continued. "Ms. Metcalf, I wish to suggest a couple of things. First, let's make an appointment to go over all of your holdings and Seth's trust fund. At that point, we'll have Mrs. Arbeson's brokerage team come in and explain her portfolio."

"Stop, just a minute," Julia said while rubbing her temples. "I'm sorry, but I'm having a little trouble wrapping my brain around this. She left me everything?"

"Yes, except the 1955 Thunderbird, Elsa's million, and the house. The Arbeson Trust was always Seth's, she merely had control over it."

"Roughly how much money are we speaking of?"

"About twenty million dollars."

Julia eyes widened and she stopped breathing. Black spots clouded her vision. A sheen of sweat broke out on her forehead. The next thing she knew she was lying on the floor with Elsa sponging her face with a damp cloth. Julia looked up at her. "Elsa, get up. You don't have to do this anymore."

Elsa smiled as tears tracked down her face. "I'd still rather have Miss Mae."

"Me, too."

CHAPTER SIXTEEN

JULIA COULDN'T SLEEP. SHE KEPT REMEMBERING the meeting. *"I'm warning you, Julia."* It kept playing through her mind like a broken record. The idea that she was in danger from Seth had seemed improbable until now. She looked at the clock, 4:15 a.m. Knowing sleep would be impossible, she got up and did three distracted miles on her treadmill.

After a hot shower and a couple cups of coffee, she decided that it was no longer too early to call Tony. His cell went to voicemail after several rings, so she left him a message. No sooner had she hit the END button when her phone beeped. It was a very groggy Tony.

"What's up, Julia?"

"I'm sorry," she said softly. "I didn't mean to wake you."

"Is everything okay?"

"Seth threatened me."

"Tell me."

She blew out a big breath and told him about the reading of the will, and Seth's outburst.

"No shit?" He went quiet.

"Tony?"

"Julia. I don't quite know how to say this, so I'll just say it." He let out a heavy sigh. "I don't think I should see you now."

Her face fell. "Why not?"

"It would be a conflict of interest. Your financial gain means I have to consider you as a person of interest."

"You mean, like a suspect?"

"I'd prefer to say, I need to clear you."

Her voice dropped to a whisper. "You know I didn't do it." Tears tracked down her face.

"Yes, I do know. But I have a job to do, and it has to be done by the book. Those who did this need to be tried and convicted. It's my job to make sure the DA has everything he needs to do that, without room for reasonable doubt as to the guilt of the assailants, the evidence presented, or the integrity of the investigation. I'm sorrier than you can ever know."

"And after?"

"I won't ask you to wait, Jule. I don't know how long it will take. Just know that I care."

"Yeah." She hung up the phone, numbly. *Shit.* She swiped away her tears impatiently.

TONY SAT AT HIS desk and ran a hand over his face. That conversation with Julia had been one of the hardest things he'd ever had to do. His phone rang. It was Welsh.

"Tony, I got some news on the hair sample you gave us."

"Yeah?"

"It's definitely not the Arbeson woman."

"Yeah?"

"It's male. DNA is in process, but that'll take a few days."

"Understood, thanks." Tony steepled his fingers and went back to his computer screen and Seth Arbeson's financials. There were a number of irregularities and cash withdrawals. He was overdrawn, his credit score was in the toilet, and he had also reported a number of valuable items stolen, claiming them on his insurance policy.

Somebody has a problem. Drugs? Alcohol? Gambling? Could be any of them, he thought.

His mind drifted to Julia. She would be cleared quickly, he was certain. But how could he risk association with her?

His phone rang again. "Lange? My office. Now." It was his boss, Captain Roark.

He walked back to the captain's office. "Yes sir?" he said, leaning against the doorjamb.

"What's this garbage I'm hearing that you went on a picnic with a wit? What in blazes is wrong with you?" His brow wrinkled.

"Well technically, she's no longer in the witness category, sir."

"She's not?"

"She just inherited Mae Arbeson's fortune."

The captain's jaw dropped. "Great. Just great. What about the kid?"

"The kid's finances are a mess. My gut tells me he purchased his stepmother's death. I think he believed he would inherit everything. According to probate records, he keeps his trust, strictly monitored by Ms. Metcalf, and the house. She got almost everything else."

"Almost?"

"The maid got a cool million and a 1955 Thunderbird."

"Must be rough."

"Ms. Metcalf's portion is estimated at roughly twenty million."

Roark whistled. "That's the one you took on the picnic?"

"That was before the reading of the will. I've, ah, put an end to the relationship."

"All the same, I'd feel better if you'd hand the case over to Johnson."

Tony sighed. "How about Melhus? He's better for this one."

"Are you in charge, or am I?"

"You are, sir. Melhus is a request only. Up to you, sir."

The captain regarded him a moment. "Fine. Melhus it is. Turn over all your notes, and for God's sake, don't be seen with the Metcalf woman until this is over."

"Yes sir."

Tony felt better not being directly involved with the case. But he still had to be careful. Seeing Julia could still give a smart attorney enough room for reasonable doubt.

Melhus had been Tony's first partner. Dale was a twenty-year veteran and the best homicide detective in the state. He'd trained more than his share of rookies, including Tony. None had meshed with Melhus as Tony had. They had become close. When Dale climbed the ladder to Detective, he nagged, pleaded, and cajoled until Tony took the Detective's exam and helped him study for it. They partnered again until budget cuts separated them, but they continued to bounce cases off one another with great success.

"Hey Dale," Tony said, poking his head into the small office occupied by the senior detective.

Dale's shoes were propped up on the corner of his tiny desk. He was perusing a book on herbal remedies. The veteran detective peered over his reading glasses and smirked."What? You got another one you can't handle by yourself? Have I taught you nothing, kid?"

"You forgot to flip your tie back down after lunch, you old fart."

"Gimme the file name." He tapped it into his tablet.

The "murder book" file held all the reports, statements, and evidence on a particular case. For a moment, he skimmed. "So what's the problem?"

"I'm turning the case over to you."

One of Melhus' eyebrows rose. "Why?"

"Conflict of interest." A slight smile played under Tony's mustache.

"Oh, sweet Jesus, boy. What have you done?"

Lange averted his eyes and tried to look sheepish. "I ah..."

"Spill."

"I took the heiress on a picnic."

"Idiot."

"I know."

Dale studied the younger man for a moment. "You got it bad?"

Tony slowly smiled. "Yeah."

"Shit. How many times I gotta tell you?"

"I know, I know."

Dale looked him up and down. "Were you dressed like that?"

"Yeah."

"Boots, too?" Melhus gestured disdainfully at Lange's worn cowboy boots.

"Yeah."

"She blind?"

"No. You know I hate strangling myself with a tie. And nobody dresses like you anymore."

"They should."

"Says you. That looks screams cop. A criminal could spot you a mile away. Who picked out that tie, anyway? You should've left it down at lunch. Spilling on it would've improved it."

Dale smiled. "Get outta here kid, and let me do my job."

64

"Thanks Dale." Tony hesitated.

"Don't worry, kid. I'll clear her first."

Tony smiled and sauntered back to his cube.

CHAPTER SEVENTEEN

JULIA FELT LIKE HER INSIDES HAD been pulled out. She tried thinking about it logically, but there was no logic in Mae's death. Tony was another issue entirely. Her brain knew that his backing off was best, but her heart ached. She was falling for him, she was sure of it.

Perhaps it was better to be apart. That would certainly give her ample opportunity to sort out the niggling doubt she had regarding her feelings. Were his feelings just a result of pity for her? Were hers a result of his having been there at a time when she needed comfort? She chewed her thumbnail in contemplation. Her reverie was broken by the phone. It was Seth.

"Julia? I was wondering if I could get an advance on my trust. My student loans are due and I need to pay them."

"Sure Seth, I'm going over to the lawyer's in the morning. How much do you need?"

"Ten thousand. I got a little behind. See, there was this girl and a great weekend in Mexico..."

"All right, I don't need to hear any more. I'll call you when I'm done at the lawyer's office and we'll meet for a coffee."

What on earth was that? And who? That kid's never been respectful, let alone friendly. Julia pondered it as she settled in for the night. *He just wants the money. But his allowance should cover that easily. Wait, Mae always said the kid had a hole in his pocket.*

She went to bed with no further thought of Seth.

It was pitch black. "Where are you?" Julia asked. A slight echo reverberated. Her words were barely a whisper.

"I'm not sure, but I'm not far away." Mae's voice seemed as though it was right next to her. Julia stretched out her arms, groping.

"I need you, Mae. How can I do this alone?" Tears choked her voice. She tried to see something, anything, in the murkiness.

"Listen to the people you trust. They're mostly the same people that I trusted." Mae's voice rose in pitch and volume. "Watch out behind you, Jule."

Julia whirled in place, frantically looking into the darkness.

"Mae? Are you still here?"

Silence.

Promptly at 9:00 the next morning, Julia was escorted into the conference room at Halberg, Finch, Lazlo, and Drew. Her hands shook even though she had taken a Xanax. All of this financial stuff had just been some mumbo jumbo language that Mae's husband spoke. Her stomach knotted. She could feel her pulse pounding in her temples. Now she would have to become fluent in legalese to do right by Mae's requests — and of course, not throw up.

The slender woman who approached Julia was much too elegant for an administrative job.

"Good Morning, Ms. Metcalf, I'm Lois Claremore," she said. Her handshake was firm, brisk, and professional. "I am

Mr. Halberg's administrative assistant. Won't you please have a seat?"

"Thanks. You wouldn't happen to have a spare cup of chamomile tea around here, would you?"

"Of course. I'll have some brewed fresh for you. It'll just take a moment."

She disappeared for a matter of seconds. When she returned, she sat near Julia.

"In a short while, we'll begin. All of those who work with the Arbeson account will attend, and we'll try to answer your questions. I'm sure you have a number of them to ask." She smiled as an intern appeared with a tray.

Julia savored the wonderful aroma as the young woman served the herbal brew in a beautiful china cup and set the tray within reach.

"May I add anything for you?" the intern inquired, smiling sweetly.

"One cream, two sugars."

She nodded and handed Julia the cup and looked at Lois. With a slight nod, Lois dismissed her.

People began to file into the conference room, and Julia began to feel a little closed in.

"Do all these people work on this account?" Julia's eyes widened. She turned to Lois.

"Yes, and more. There are a great many facets to Mrs. Arbeson's personal holdings and Seth Arbeson's trust."

"I'm really in over my head."

Lois smiled. "You'll get the hang of it. I'm sure you remember Mr. Halberg? He is the corporate attorney to your holdings."

For the next two hours, the staff brought Julia up to date on the holdings of Mae Arbeson. After Julia signed all the necessary papers, she rubbed her aching temples. Numbers and margins and speculations all danced wildly in her brain.

There were so many terms she didn't fully understand. Within that time, she had filled half of a legal pad with questions and points for clarification. Resolving those took another three hours. When everyone finally stopped talking, she looked around the table. "Are we finished?"

"Yes, with the holdings. Next we have the Arbeson Trust," Lois said, grabbing another binder full of papers.

"Can we schedule something later? My head just won't hold any more."

"Let's take a short break," Mr. Halberg interjected. "I promise you the Arbeson Trust won't take more than fifteen minutes."

"Really? Fifteen minutes? Let's get it done then. Pass the tea."

"There are a few papers for you to sign. Basically, the way it works is that Seth Arbeson gets an allotment from the trust monthly. That's automatic, and you don't have to do anything. But, if Seth requests additional funds, it will have to go through you. This gives you the opportunity and the responsibility to investigate the reasons for any additional disbursement.

"Oh that's right! Seth wanted me to get him an extra $10,000. He ran short and needs to pay his student loans."

Mr. Halberg stared at her for a moment. "Ms. Metcalf, Seth has no student loans. He would have no need for them. His educational fund pays for all books, tuitions, and expenses. However, he has not chosen to attend college, although he did sign up for a course once."

"Why, that sneaky little rat."

"I'm sure Mrs. Arbeson had good reason to leave the Arbeson Trust under your care, and you'll know what to do. Her will specified that Seth's trust was to be monitored until such time as you decide that he is capable and responsible enough to handle it himself."

"Sounds like that will be when hell freezes."

Lois handed her the papers to sign and helped her arrange them into a binder.

At long last, Lois showed her to the door. "I know we've thrown a lot at you today, and you will likely have more questions."

"I'll call you and set up an appointment."

"Very well."

CHAPTER EIGHTEEN

TONY SAT IN HIS CAR JUST down the block from Julia's. He'd spent several hours each of the last few days watching her, and had even checked her house when she wasn't home.

She pulled up into the driveway. Papers and books were stacked high in her arms. She looked weary. He longed to jump out and help her, but it was best for the case that they not be seen together. His heart ached. Why couldn't he control it? Shove it back down in the darkness of his soul, where it belonged?

Dale was Tony's best friend. His counsel was sacrosanct. He was always there for Tony, no matter the circumstances. Lange sighed. Julia had crawled into his heart. He dialed Melhus' number.

"Yeah, Melhus here."

"Dale, I need some advice."

"Fifty bucks on Tranquil Evening in the fourth to win."

"Very funny."

"What have you done now, boy?"

"Why do you always assume it's something bad?"

Dale waited.

"Okay, this is personal."

"Yes, my son?"

"I think I'm in love."

Dale sighed. "The Metcalf woman?"

"Yeah."

"Bad timing."

"Yeah."

"Don't get caught, not even by me." The phone went dead.

JULIA UNLOCKED THE FRONT door, and rushed inside as the phone began to ring. She snatched it up just before it went to voice mail.

"Julia?"

"Seth, hi. Give me one sec." She put down her load of papers and books. "Okay," she said.

"Did you get my advance?"

"I was going to call you about that. You don't have any student loans. I'm not stupid, Seth."

"Look. I need the money, and I need it today. Get it for me." His tone was controlled and insistent.

"Seth, it's very simple. You give me a good — and I stress the word *good* — reason, and I will decide whether to release the funds to you."

Seth's breathing became fierce. "No, Julia. You don't decide. I do. And you'll do as I say. I have Arbeson blood in my veins. You don't. Now get me that money."

"How dare you speak to me that way, Seth?" Her blood pressure rose several notches. Her teeth gritted as anger twisted her gut. "Your mother wanted me to look out for you since you obviously can't do it for yourself. And that's exactly what I'm going to do. The answer is no."

"That woman wasn't my mother. She was stubborn too, at first."

"What are you saying? Did you hurt her?"

"I'm not a complete asshole."

"The answer is still no."

"You'll change your mind." His voice was even, but something about the way he said it made a chill run up her spine.

"This conversation is over." The button to disconnect eluded her shaking fingers until the third try.

JULIA TOOK OFF HER readers and rubbed her tired eyes as she finished poring over the information on Mae's legacy for a third time. It was impossible to understand. She sighed and got up to take her empty supper plate to the kitchen and refill her teacup. The herbal tea she preferred had a wonderfully spicy aroma. Cinnamon filled her nostrils. She closed her eyes and rubbed the back of her aching neck.

The sound of the doorbell startled her. A flower truck was parked out in front and a man in coveralls stood on her front stoop. A grin spread across her face as she opened the door. It must've been Tony.

"Julia Metcalf?"

"Yes," she replied happily.

He shoved her back into the house and threw the flowers to the floor. The door slammed behind him, and he grabbed her arm, twisted it around, and pinned her up against the wall. She drew in a breath to scream, but cut it short when a gun appeared close to her face. The cold metal pressed against her neck, and the man's other hand covered her mouth. He leaned up against her and hissed in her face. "Shut up. One sound and I use this, understand?"

Eyes wide and breath puffing through her nose, she nodded carefully. He eased up slightly and said, "Now that we understand each other, we're gonna have a talk." His breath stank of cigarettes and decay.

The color drained from her face and her knees turned to water. He pushed harder.

"No, you aren't going to pass out. Do you hear me?" But he did move her away from the door and pivoted around, holding her from the back while keeping the gun pressed up under her jaw. "I'm going to need you to get some of that Arbeson money. See, your little buddy Seth owes a lot. Since you're in charge of his trust, you're going to see that it's paid."

She tried to act casual. "Well, why didn't you say so? Sure, how much are we talking about?" Her voice shook and her gut roiled. Bile bubbled up the back of her throat.

"He's down twenty five grand, with 2% interest compounding daily. Then there's my collection fee, so..." The man was cut off when the door burst open.

"Police, freeze!" Officers appeared from the front and rear of the house.

His grip tightened. "Back off or I'll kill her." He barely got the words out when he started to convulse, having been hit from behind by a Taser. The barrel of the pistol scraped against her neck as he went down in a heap, pulling a side table and lamp down with him. An officer materialized at her side. "Are you all right, ma'am?"

"Yes, I think so." A wave of dizziness swept over her.

"Whoa, you'd better sit down." The officer took her elbow and guided her to the couch.

"How did you know to come?" she asked.

"Must've been one of your neighbors. We got an anonymous call."

An EMT wrapped a blanket around her shoulders. "Would you be more comfortable laying down? You may be in shock." He took her blood pressure and checked her breathing and pupil reaction.

"No, I'm okay. Just a little shaky."

"Is your stomach upset?"

"Um, I don't think so."

He took her pulse. "Strong pulse, but I'd still like you to lay down for just a few minutes. Please."

She stretched out on the sofa and put her feet up on the arm. The EMT cleaned the scratches on her neck and asked her if she wanted a counselor to talk to. She shook her head. "I'll be fine. I just need a few minutes."

"Is there somewhere you can stay tonight?" the patrolman asked.

"I, I guess I could get a hotel room." Her mind felt sluggish and her heart was still racing.

The EMT smiled. "I could get you a room at St. Bart's. And I have a nice comfy ambulance to get you there. It would probably be a good idea. The doctors should at least look you over."

She nodded vaguely. Try as she might, her hands would not stop shaking.

"Is there someone I can call for you?"

For a moment, she just stared. "No, there's no one anymore."

The EMT opened a package and reached for her arm.

"What are you doing?"

"Starting an IV. That and a heart monitor are standard protocol given your symptoms."

"All that just because I'm shaky?"

He smiled. "And pale, and sweaty; need I say more?"

She shook her head.

THE EMERGENCY ROOM DOCTOR examined her and read the EMT's findings. "You're going to have a nasty bruise on your neck, but otherwise, you're physically fine. I'm concerned about your emotional state. You still look a bit pale and shaky."

"I...I think I'm okay."

The doctor looked around the curtain at the rest of the ER. "Look," she said, turning back to Julia. "Stay here for a while and rest. I'll look in on you when I can. I'll also boot you out if we need the space. Deal?"

Julia nodded. She felt drained. At least here, she was safe.

CHAPTER NINETEEN

A FEW HOURS LATER, JULIA CAUGHT a cab from St. Bart's to a nearby hotel. Once the security system was installed, she moved back home. Despite the fact that the security firm assured Julia that no one could get into the house without her knowledge, the butterflies in her stomach wouldn't be still. The police would be called automatically should the system not be disarmed within thirty seconds of entry. They had installed keypads at the entrances and sensors at all the windows.

Resigned, she took a sleeping pill and lay down in her bed but her eyes remained wide open. In an attempt to relax, she opened a book, but only stared at the words.

Her bedroom door was locked, and lights burned all over the house. One bedroom window was opened just a bit, to let in the cool night air. She lay awake for much longer than it should take to fall into a drug-induced sleep.

It came as quite a surprise to her when she woke up screaming. Her hands shook so badly that she couldn't write the fragments of the dream that she could remember. She only knew it was bad, and it was about Mae. Something deep inside her told her that it would help the police to know what was in the dream. Tears began to roll down her cheeks as her stomach clenched, and her heart ached mercilessly.

When daylight finally started to color the sky in purple and orange streaks, she unlocked her bedroom door and padded to the kitchen. Her eyes were puffy and red, and her chin still quivered periodically. She fought the unease inside of her. As if on autopilot, she measured coffee and water, and sat down to wait for it to drip.

The soft knock on her back door sent her flying to her feet. Heart pounding, she grabbed a butcher knife from the block and crept toward the door.

"Who's there?" she yelled.

"It's me, Tony." He spoke in hushed tones.

Her shoulders relaxed as she disarmed the security system and opened the door, but her fist was still clenched tightly around the hilt of the knife.

"Whoa," he said as he slid his hand over her fist and gently removed the knife from it. "Rough night?" He placed the blade on the counter and cupped her cheeks in his hands.

With a slight nod, she broke down.

"Hey, it's okay," he whispered as he drew her in and held her until the tears stopped.

"Don't play with me, Tony."

He paused, debating the timing of his response. He tipped her face up to meet his gaze. "I realize that I've hurt you. I'm sorry. I just didn't see any other way to get Mae's killer without screwing it up so that he goes free."

"Why are you here?"

He looked at his boots. "I've been keeping an eye on you since the will was read." He couldn't look her in the eye.

"You have?" A slow smile crept across her face as her

hand grazed his cheek.

"I've been here most nights. I'm the one who called in the flower guy. It took every ounce of willpower I had not to knock on this door. But then I realized I couldn't stay away, and that this conversation ought to be face to face." He slid his arms around her.

She shifted her hand around to the back of his neck, and her lips brushed his. "So now the case is screwed up?"

He smiled. "Not yet."

"But you said…"

"I handed over the case."

Her eyes widened. "But why?"

"Julia, I just couldn't leave you unprotected. And, I've been thinking about a career change. The plant at the edge of town offered me a position as head of security. I'm giving it serious consideration."

"You would do that for me?"

"Yes, and I would do it for me."

She told him what she could about the dream and about the strange happenings of the past couple of days. He dialed his cell when she finished.

"Dale? It's Tony. I have some more info on the Arbeson case. And I want a squad parked in front of Julia Metcalf's place 24/7. She's been getting threats."

He listened for a few minutes, furrowing his brow. "Are you sure?" Tony shot a glance at Julia. "Okay, I'll bring her with me."

"What was that last bit?" she asked.

"Melhus says he has come across evidence implicating you in Mae's murder. Come with me and we'll clear it up."

THEY CAUGHT UP WITH Detective Sergeant Dale Melhus in the Homicide Department. He was on his way to the commander's office when they walked in.

"Dale," Tony called after him.

Melhus turned around and strode toward them. "This must be Ms. Metcalf," he said. "I have some questions for you. If you'll come with me?"

He led them to an interview room. "Tony, you'll have to wait out here. You know the drill."

Tony nodded as Melhus led Julia into the room and closed the door.

Julia looked around. "Isn't there usually a mirror thing where people can sit and watch you interview me?"

"Not this room," Melhus answered, smiling without humor. "Please, sit. Can I get you something? A coffee, perhaps?"

"No, thanks. What's this all about?"

"Okay, we'll get right to it. You are the heir to the Arbeson fortune, aren't you?"

"No. I inherited Mae Langford Arbeson's holdings. The Arbeson Trust belongs to Seth Arbeson."

"But you control the Trust?"

"Yes, but only until Seth can handle it himself."

"Which will be when?"

"When I have determined that he can handle it responsibly."

"So, in effect, you own that as well?"

"No, I haven't any reason to touch the Trust and I can't make any withdrawals."

"Don't you draw a salary as Trustee?"

"It was set up that way, but I refused it. I don't need the money. I wish I didn't have the money. I wish I had Mae."

Melhus smirked. "Ms. Metcalf, where were you on the night Mrs. Arbeson was murdered?"

The shock of the question left her speechless for a moment.

"I was at home. I went to bed early with a headache. I woke up about 1:30 a.m. and called Mae. She wasn't answering her phone, so I called the house line. Seth answered and he told me she was gone. So I got in my car and went over to check."

He placed his hands on the small, scarred table and leaned into her personal space. "So you have no one to corroborate your alibi?"

"I was at home, as I said."

"How did you know there had been foul play?"

"I didn't for sure, I just had a... I guess you'd call it a hunch."

"A hunch?" Dale's eyebrows shot up as he stood to his full height. "You get up in the middle of the night and go traipsing across town on a hunch?"

"My hunches have proven to be pretty accurate."

"If you had say, hired someone to dispose of Mrs. Arbeson, that would account for your prior knowledge, wouldn't it?"

Tears filled her eyes. "I get it that you don't know how close Mae and I were, but she was my dearest friend on this earth. I loved her with all my heart." Julia wiped her eyes.

"Tell me the truth, Ms. Metcalf. You knew that you would inherit her fortune, didn't you?"

"I had no idea." Tears choked her as she fought for control.

"I think a night in the county lock up might refresh your memory."

He seemed angry now, and Julia didn't know what to say to convince him of her innocence.

"Turn off the tears, lady. They don't work on me."

"But I didn't... I couldn't. I loved her like a sister. We

were probably closer than most sisters." *What is wrong with this man? More importantly, why isn't he looking for Mae's killer?* "Can I see Tony now?"

"No. We're not even close to done."

"Why are you treating me this way? I didn't kill her, and I didn't arrange to have it done. I never wanted her damn money, don't you get it?"

"You have no alibi. Your fingerprints are all over the Arbeson house, and you inherited everything. Who's the one who doesn't get it?"

"We were friends since childhood — of course my fingerprints are all over her house. Are you going to arrest me?"

"I haven't decided."

"Do I need a lawyer?"

"I don't know, do you? If you're innocent, and that's a big if right now, I wouldn't think you'd need one, but lady, I need the truth out of you. Right now."

"I have told you the truth." Her hands were shaking.

The interrogation went on for two hours, with Melhus asking roughly the same questions over and over. Finally, when Melhus could get nothing further from her, he let her go home, with the warning that he was to be apprised of her whereabouts at all times.

Tony was waiting when she came out of the interrogation room. "Are you okay?"

"No. Please take me home."

When they got to the car, Julia began to cry. "He kept asking me why I killed her."

Tony handed her his handkerchief and patted her knee. "It's pretty standard, given the circumstances."

Her head whipped around, and she shot an indignant look in his direction. "I can't believe you people treat innocent folk so poorly, and accuse them of terrible things they couldn't possibly do."

"Not everyone is innocent, and some people lie." He rubbed her arm. "The most effective way to trip them up is to ask them for the story over and over, from different angles and see if the story changes. Melhus is a good cop. He's doing his job. He'll track down the killer. Don't let it upset you."

"Oh, sure. That'll be simple." She threw her hands up and dabbed at her eyes and nose.

"Tell me about the dream. The one that upset you."

"I wish I could, but I don't remember. I can't shake the feeling that there are important details that would help, but I've tried as hard as I can. I just can't remember."

He paused. "The dreams aren't admissible as evidence, Jule."

"I know, but there's something, I just know it." She studied his face for a moment.

"Think about this a minute," he suggested. "We have a psychologist we use that specializes in hypnosis. She might be able to help you remember the details."

"I'll think about it. Not to change the subject, but I thought we couldn't be seen together?"

"You're right. Once I drop you off from this official police business, we'll have to be very careful."

CHAPTER TWENTY

"Jule? I'm sorry. I didn't know." Mae's voice was barely a whisper.

"Of course you didn't, Mae."

A dragon sat near them, dozing contently. Julia kept her eye on it as she spoke. "What happens if we awaken him?" She asked quietly, nodding in the scaly thing's direction.

Mae shuddered in response.

Suddenly, a door opened and Seth appeared. He laughed as he yelled, "We can't allow quiet! We must have noise."

He started banging a pot with a large metal spoon. Mae and Julia ran toward him as the dragon stood up and shot fire from his enormous fanged mouth, lashing out with his long muscular tail.

"Seth, let us out of here," Mae begged.

"I want my money. It's all mine now. All of it."

"That thing will kill us. Let us out, please."

"And I'll be dead without it. Goodbye, Mae. Goodbye, Julia." *He laughed again and slammed the door. They heard the lock click into place.*

Julia and Mae turned around to face the beast. It roared ferociously and swiped a large claw in their direction. Its red eyes glowed ominously as they backed up into the corner of the room clutching one another. It slinked closer, as if sizing them up. Baring its long fangs, a ribbon of bright flame erupted from its throat. It locked eyes with Mae's and sprang. Julia grabbed the door and pulled as hard as she could.

The door suddenly opened, and Julia heard Mae call out. "Run, Jule! I'm right behind you."

Outside, Julia found herself in a dense forest. There was no moon to guide her steps, so she felt around the rough terrain with her bare feet.

The dragon's fiery eyes peered at her in the dark. "You're doomed," its menacing voice growled.

She started to run. The rough terrain of the forest floor sliced at her legs and ankles. She was so busy looking behind her, that she didn't see the precipice until it was too late. Her feet tried to back pedal, but she still toppled over the edge. Grasping at anything she could, she closed her hand like a vise around a small branch that protruded through the rocks.

Gulping great breaths of air, she hugged the cliff face. Her face and arms ached from the bruises and scrapes. Suddenly, she heard the dragon's raspy grunts. Her breathing all but stopped and her eyes grew wide. Small pebbles rained down on her as it reached the edge of the cliff.

Pressing her body flat against the rocks, she heard it start to laugh. It was an evil, guttural sound. Tears sprang to her eyes, and she prayed for salvation. One of its claws lashed into the flesh on her back. Searing pain blinded her momentarily, and the claws struck again.

This time, she could not hold on any longer, and her hands slipped off the branch. As her body plummeted into the darkness, she let loose an agonizing scream. But even that didn't drown out the laughter of the terrible beast.

She awoke with her arms flailing in the dark. Even with the fresh breeze that fluttered the curtains at the slightly open window, she felt like she was suffocating. It slowly dawned on her that it had all been a dream. Someone pounded on the door and called her name. After a moment, she recognized it as Tony.

It only took a moment to disarm the alarm, get to the door, unlock the two locks, remove the chain, and fling open the door.

"Julia! Are you all right?" His panicked voice squeaked as he looked her over, and then pulled her in close. "I heard you screaming. It scared the hell out of me."

He looked into her eyes, and kissed her as gently as he could. His arms came around her and held on tight. She grabbed him and kissed him hard. Everything she'd been feeling swam in a circle around her heart. She began to unbutton his shirt.

He put a hand over hers. "I can't do this now. It wouldn't be right."

She looked into his eyes. The conflict he felt showed. "I need comfort tonight, Tony, and intimacy. I'm a big girl. I understand all the risks of what I'm asking." She smiled slightly with hope in her eyes.

He leaned in and kissed her. "You're sure about this?"

"Yes." She resumed unbuttoning his shirt and ran her hands over his lean chest. He let her take the lead; go as far as she wanted, if she wanted.

Gently, he caressed her shoulders and kissed her neck.

"Touch me," she whispered. "I need to feel you against my skin." She tugged at her nightshirt.

He pushed her hands away. His hands ran around to her back and stroked her lightly while he kissed her more deeply. She shivered, and he stopped.

"Are you okay?" he whispered. "I'll stop if you want me

to."

"Don't you dare."

"I'm glad you said that. I wasn't sure I could."

Her nightshirt was on the floor in a heartbeat. He backed her up to the dinette table and lifted her onto it then stepped between her legs. Kisses and his nimble tongue sent electrical charges straight to her abdomen. She grabbed for his pants and tried to unfasten them. He caught her hands and held them.

"Not yet," he whispered hoarsely.

"Oh please, I want you."

"Soon," he said as he tongued her erect nipple. He circled his hands under her bottom and lifted her close. She wrapped her legs around his hips.

"Which way?" he said.

"Upstairs, first door on the right." She nipped his shoulder lightly and kissed his neck.

Her bed was an old fashioned four-poster, not that either of them noticed. Clothing was discarded and lay in a heap on the floor. They lay intertwined on the bed kissing and caressing. She put her hand on his chest.

"What's wrong, Julia?"

"I, ah... I haven't done this in a long, long time."

He grinned. "You haven't lost your touch, I assure you."

It was only a couple minutes later that they were simultaneously flung into ecstasy. Panting and sweating, they clung to each other afterwards with a need neither had ever known before.

Tony pulled her close with her head on his shoulder and their hands clasped. They fell asleep in each other's arms.

Tony awoke in the darkness wondering if it had been a dream. He turned over full of anticipation. She lay sleeping next to him and a smile crept across his face.

He longed to touch her face as it relaxed in sleep. Her

mouth curved slightly upward making him wonder what she was dreaming. Her gold and silver hair was splayed across her pillow like flowing silk. His fingertips stroked some of the strands that lay close to him.

Propped up on his elbow, he watched her slumber in the moonlight. Tony wondered why it was that he'd never felt this way about a woman before. Sure, he'd been in love with his ex-wife once upon a time, but this all-consuming feeling that he had for Julia was new and compelling.

Julia opened her eyes, and smiled at him then glanced away.

"Okay, I'll bite. What were you dreaming?"

Even in the dim light, he could see her cheeks redden. "I can't say, and I'm not writing it down. You'll think I'm a kook."

"You mean you *won't* say," he replied as he laid his head on the pillow and reached for her cheek.

"It was about us. That's all I'm going to tell you."

"Hmm. Were we doing something fun?"

She giggled. "Yes."

"Something like this?" he asked, as he dove onto her and began to kiss her neck and face ferociously.

Laughter erupted from her as he worked his mouth over her skin. His primal grunting noises made her giggle all the more. After a moment, his kisses became tender. His eyes met hers and held for a long moment.

"I love you, Julia."

She smiled and gazed into his eyes. "I was never one to believe in love at first sight, until now. I love you, Tony." Her arms and legs snaked their way around him and held on tight.

"Tell me your dream," he murmured.

TONY GOT UP BEFORE dawn to shower and dress then sat next to her on the bed. "I have to go," he said quietly.

She nodded. "Will you call me later?" Worry creased her brow, though she tried in vain to sound casual.

"Every time I get a chance." His kiss was tender and sincere.

CHAPTER TWENTY-ONE

DR. INGVALDSON HAD A LONG HISTORY with the police department. She had helped witnesses remember the tiny details and counseled those traumatized by being the victim of, or witnessing, a terrible crime.

Julia found the woman likeable and opened up to her immediately.

"Julia, I'm fascinated by precognitive dreams. Do you journal them?" the doctor asked. She folded her hands in her lap. Her serene face wore a smile, both comforting, and strong.

"Meticulously. In fact, I'm a bit obsessive about it."

"And do you record the reality, as well?"

"Yes. Most of the time the dreams are full of symbolism. I have to try and figure out what it meant afterward by comparing it to reality. On rare occasion, they're straight facts."

"Has there ever been a time, such as this, when you couldn't remember the details of the dream?"

"Sure. Most of the time I remember the details for a short time, which is why I write them down. The details fade fast."

"That's perfectly normal."

"This dream, all I remember is waking up completely terrified, knowing the dream was about Mae. I can't shake the feeling that there are details that would be helpful to the police in catching her murderer."

"Yes, that may be true. I'm going to first get you into a very relaxed state, and then I will suggest that you simply give me straight reporting without emotion or opinion."

"I must warn you, however, that when you are brought back to higher consciousness, you will likely be distraught. I have a medication for that, should you need it."

"I don't want anything unless it's really bad. Is that okay?"

"As you wish. Now, lie back and get comfortable. Close your eyes and listen only to the sound of my voice…"

Julia listened to the doctor's voice until it faded away. Then there was nothing. Just blackness. She became aware of moisture on her face that was both warm and cold. Her heart pounded and her breath came in raspy puffs.

She slowly opened her eyes and found herself in a wine cellar that was cool and slightly damp. She realized that she was seeing it just as Mae had a few weeks before. Her foot throbbed. Mae hoped that the big ape who'd manhandled her was still clutching his crotch.

Two hours earlier, Mae had been snug in her bed, sound asleep. A huge callused hand muffled her cries before they escaped her lips. She tried to bite the hand, but wasn't able to sink her teeth in. Her arms flailed, and she grabbed a handful of hair. He gathered her hands up with his free hand and pinned them to the headboard. She dropped the hairs she'd pulled out as she tried to kick, but the momentum was swallowed up by the satin sheets she favored and the eider down duvet.

He bound her wrists together with duct tape. It pulled at her skin. He dragged her from the bed exerting almost no effort. Her knees banged the floor, sending a jolt up her spine. He hoisted her to her feet as a wave of dizziness swept over her and her legs buckled momentarily.

"Go ahead and faint," he said with a menacing grin. "It'll make my job easier."

She fought it, knowing that losing consciousness could well mean her death. Her whole body felt like water. He wrestled her out to the van that was parked in the sweeping circular drive and loosened his grip for a moment to fumble for his keys.

Mae seized the opportunity. She slammed her foot into his crotch with every ounce of strength she had. He doubled over and groaned loudly, but his vise-like grip only tightened, instead of loosening. As he slowly unfolded, his fist came around and connected with her left eye.

Blinding pain exploded and bright lights flashed in her head as she leaned against the van motionless. A scream died in her throat as the second blow struck her sharply from the other side. Blackness folded into her vision.

Her head throbbed like a ten-pound hammer on an anvil. Slowly her right eye opened. The left was swollen shut. The black bag over her head sent her into an instant claustrophobic panic. Her first impulse was to tear it from her head, but her hands wouldn't move. The duct tape that held her in place bit into her wrists and ankles.

"Mrs. Arbeson, how lovely to have you as my guest." Her head jerked in the direction of the voice. As he pulled the bag from her head, she became nearly giddy with relief. "That's better now, isn't it?" He carefully smoothed her disheveled hair with his meticulously manicured hand. This man had a curled mustache and meticulously swirled hair, what was left of it.

"What do you want?" Mae hissed.

"You understand that your stepson owes me a great deal

of money, don't you?"

"What has that to do with me?"

He worked his hands into a pair of black fitted gloves and picked up a leather sap. He weighed it carefully in his hands. "My dear woman, it has everything to do with you. You control the Arbeson Trust."

"There's nothing I can or will do to change that."

"Oh, I think you'll change your mind." He smiled humorlessly. He laid the sap carefully in his hand and showed it to Mae. "Are you familiar with this item, Mrs. Arbeson?"

Her eyes widened, but never left the object.

"It's called a sap. This one belonged to my father, Anthony Cordell. It has its own story:

"Albert?" Anthony Cordell asked.

"Yes, Father?" The ten-year-old stared up at Anthony. He knew what this was about. He prepared as best he could for what surely would be a severe punishment.

"Your mother tells me you've been untidy. And you've neglected your studies despite her requests for you to do your homework. Is this true?"

Albert's eyes cast downward.

"Answer me." Anthony's voiced tensed.

"Yes, Father. But I only forgot to make up my bed once, and I was going to pick up my clothes." Albert's voice was barely above a whisper.

"You're a smart boy, but you lack discipline."

Albert sniffed.

Anthony laid a hand on Albert's shoulder and sighed. "Come to the workshop with me. Perhaps if I teach you a trade, you'll not be so inclined to disappoint your mother."

Albert's heart sang. Never before had his father suggested such a thing. Normally, it was swift and terrible retribution for his misgivings.

"Sit on the stool and watch." His father's voice remained even.

Albert nodded and eagerly tracked his every move. Anthony cut a piece of thick leather with a heavy pair of snippers. He fashioned a rectangle of sorts, with a long slight taper on one end. On the other, he rounded the corners taking care that when the two sides were folded inward they matched.

"Albert, take this punch, and make holes along the edges where I have marked. Do you see?" He showed him the piece.

"Yes, Father." The marks made a U, leaving a few inches of untouched leather on the tapered end.

Albert worked with the punch and hammer. His holes were uniform and exactly where his father wanted them.

While he worked, Anthony cut a piece of three-quarter-inch dowel about four inches long. He whittled it into the form of a rough handle.

"Look, Father!" Albert held up the leather rectangle now dotted with a line of small exacting holes.

"That's a fine job, Albert." Anthony smiled.

"Take this leather thong and thread it through the holes."

Albert's eager hands stitched the leather together to form an eight-inch-long tube closed at the rounded end.

"Not so tight," Anthony admonished.

"Yes Father."

"Leave the strings hanging."

Albert nodded.

"Now, give it to me," Anthony said as Albert finished.

"What are we making, Father?"

"It's called a sap." Anthony filled the tube with lead shot that he emptied from several shotgun shells. When it was full, Anthony weighed it carefully in his hands. With a nod, he inserted the handle, and tied the remaining length of the thong in a crisscross pattern. Several times, he stopped and wrapped his fingers around it, and adjusted for fit.

"Now," Anthony said. "Can you guess the purpose of our sap?" A smile grew on Anthony's face.

"No." Albert's voice was small and meek. His eyes grew wide.

"I think you can, Albert." He edged closer to the boy. "You shall never, ever disappoint your mother again."

Albert came back to the present.

"It's made of the finest leather and is filled with lead shot. I can tell you from bitter experience that it's quite painful to be on the receiving end."

"So you think you can literally beat a signature out of me?" Her voice shook.

"Not if I don't have to. I've had the paperwork drawn up, and all you need do is sign. Really, Mrs. Arbeson, this needn't be difficult." He stood primly holding the sap as though it were something he didn't even wish to touch let alone use. "Lon, untie Mrs. Arbeson's right hand." Lon did as he was told, and Mae used the opportunity to stretch her arm and fingers. Cordell held out a gold pen.

She stared at it for just a beat. "Ah, I'm left handed."

The impact from the back of his hand was far more painful than she had anticipated, but her anger rushed past the pain. She spat in his face. He stopped cold, and closed his eyes as revulsion spread over his face. He pulled a neatly folded handkerchief from his pocket and wiped the saliva from his cheek.

She smiled, feeling some small satisfaction.

His fist connected with her jaw with such force that the chair nearly toppled over. The entire side of her face felt as though it had been pulverized.

"How disgusting," he said. "I expected better manners from someone of your social station, Mrs. Arbeson."

"Look Mister," she slurred through her barely opened jaws. "I can't give you what you want." When the sap struck her side she doubled over, gasping for air.

"All I need for you to do, Mrs. Arbeson, is sign the trust over to Seth. That's all I want. You'll have plenty left."

"It's not my trust. It's Seth's." She heard the crunch of bone at the next blow. Instinctively, her body leaned to protect her broken ribs. Breathing was excruciating now.

"This is your last chance Mrs. Arbeson. The trust. Now."

She slowly straightened up despite the searing pain. With her one good eye, she stared him down. "Shove it up your ass. How's that for manners?" The swelling around her jaw and cheek made her smile hideous. Albert's eyes burned with anger.

"Lon. Remove Mrs. Arbeson and take her on a walk in the woods." His words were clipped and impatient.

Lon nodded. "Yes, Mr. Cordell."

"One way or another, Mrs. Arbeson, Seth will control the trust." He laughed as Lon dragged her painfully from the cellar.

He hadn't bothered to blindfold her. She knew she wasn't coming back. *You'll pay*, she thought.

They drove for some time, to a wooded area far north of either estate. *They'll never find me here*, she thought sadly.

"Don't give me no trouble, lady," the big man said as he dragged her from the car.

"Hang on," she said bending over. "Just let me have a minute to catch my breath."

In that moment, she gathered every last ounce of strength she could muster. She lunged at Lon, pushing him as hard as she could and ran for the road. He backpedaled then regrouped as he took off after her. With her inability to straighten up or breathe properly, she was no match for Lon's long legs. He caught her as she tried to climb the side of the ditch up to the road.

"You shouldna done that," Lon told her. His unrelenting grip bruised her arm as he dragged her back to the woods. She struggled, but he hit her and she fell. He threw her over his shoulder and carried her far into the thicket.

When he stopped, he flung her to the ground. She landed in a painful heap.

"Please, your name is Lon, right? Look Lon, you don't have to do this," she begged. She struggled to her feet for the last time.

He pulled a pistol from under his jacket.

"No," she cried as she launched herself toward him. Her nails raked deeply down the side of his face. There was a loud boom and all went black.

Julia's sobs racked her body as Dr. Ingvaldson awakened her.

"I've given you a sedative, Julia. You were very agitated, even through my suggestions. I'm so very sorry for your loss. I can help you cope with this..."

Darkness overtook her again.

CHAPTER TWENTY-TWO

DETECTIVE MELHUS TWIRLED THE TOOTHPICK FROM one side of his mouth to the other as he examined the financial records of Mae Arbeson's estate with a great deal of frustration. He had already forwarded copies of them to the appropriate members of the forensics team, but had hoped to glean something from going over them himself.

I'm not stupid, he thought. *But this is more complicated than an IRS form that falls under the heading of the Paperwork Reduction Act.*

He threw up his hands and shut down his laptop in exasperation. He pitched the splintered shards of the toothpick into the trash. It was a poor substitute for the Marlboro he craved. He'd been off the coffin nails for eight days, twelve hours, forty-two minutes, and a handful of seconds. He pulled on his jacket and reached into his breast pocket to retrieve another spearmint-flavored toothpick as he pushed open the door and headed for his car.

"Hey Dale." His head swiveled in the direction of the

greeting.

"What's new, Tony?" Melhus smiled for the first time in hours.

"Living' the dream, my friend. How's the Arbeson case shaping up?"

"You know I can't discuss it with you, Tony. You're off the case for a reason."

"Just between us, Dale. Come on."

"No can do. But I will tell you that the case is ongoing, and all leads are being investigated." A grin split Dale's face as he quoted the overly used line that was fed to the press when they asked such questions. "Are you getting any, or have you been stupid for absolutely no reason at all?"

Tony smiled. "She's great, Dale. I'm keeping my distance, but the minute this case is sewed up? I'm going to take her to Très Chic for dinner. Maybe even ask her to marry me."

"Way too soon," Dale opined. "Play a little hard to get, will ya? Besides, what if she's implicated?"

"Is she?"

"It's just a what-if question."

Tony smirked. "In that case, I should consider a trip to Brazil."

It was Dale's turn to smirk. "Gotta go, Lange. You take care."

TWENTY MINUTES LATER, DALE stood waiting for Jeffrey Metcalf to answer his front door. When at last it opened, Jeff stood before him in lounge pants rubbing his eyes. "Yeah?"

Dale flipped open the case that held his badge. "Detective Sergeant Dale Melhus. Jeffrey Metcalf?"

Jeff's brow furrowed. "Yeah?" His voice took on a

suspicious tone.

"May I come in? I'd like to talk to you about your former spouse, Julia Metcalf, and her friend, Mae Arbeson."

"Oh yeah, right. I saw on the news that Mae was dead. Come on in. I'm having a beer. Want one?"

"No thanks, I never indulge before noon."

"Right. It's not how it looks. I work nights, so really, it's like five o'clock for me."

"I'm not here to discuss your drinking habits, Mr. Metcalf."

"Right. What do you want to know?"

"How well do you get along with your ex-wife?"

"Julia? Yeah, we get along fine now."

"Now? How do you mean?"

"Well, you know. We got divorced. If you're getting along, you don't get divorced."

"How long has it been?"

"Um… yeah. It's been eleven years."

Dale rubbed at his nose to hide the smile that tempted his lips. "I understand Julia and Mrs. Arbeson had been friends for many years."

"Yeah, they were pretty tight."

"Did Julia ever mention being an heir to the Arbeson fortune?"

"Really? How much did she get?"

"I don't know, but Mrs. Arbeson left everything to her except a million dollars and her T-Bird."

"Wow, for sure I'd have stuck around if I'd known. Know what I mean?" He laughed.

"You don't think Julia knew then?"

"Probably not, but she liked having a rich friend. They were always shopping, and Mae would buy her stuff. In fact, Mae paid Julia's lawyer when we got divorced."

"So she liked what that money could buy her."

"Wait a sec. Is Julia a suspect?"

"I'm trying to cover all the bases, that's all."

"Well, for sure she was into the money thing, but I really don't think she'd kill Mae."

Dale got to his feet and smiled. "I think that's all I'll need for now, Mr. Metcalf."

He stuck out his hand. Jeff shook it and followed him to the door. Dale stopped just short and turned to face Jeff.

"By the way, you'd best get rid of that cannabis plant in your kitchen window. I'll bet you could see it from the alleyway."

"Oh man. I thought you were cool." He turned, put his hands behind his back, and waited. Dale merely chuckled as the shut the door behind him.

Dale's next stop was at the home of Phyllis Watcomb, Julia's neighbor.

"Oh Detective," she said, pawing at her hair. "I don't know her well. I mind my own business."

Melhus knew from experience that anytime someone uttered those words, it was probably as far from the truth as one could get. He waited for her to continue.

"She's a very strange woman. One night, she came running over in the middle of the night babbling something about a dream she had. She said a snake was winding around my purse. Well, I had no idea what she was up to, so I slammed the door right in her face. But the next day, someone stole my wallet. I think she must have known something about it.

"Sometimes, I see her lights go on late at night, and she writes in a diary or something, and then the lights go out.

"I heard she was friends with that rich woman who was killed. Is that true?" She cocked an ear in his direction as though she didn't want to miss a word.

"Yes, they were friends. Do you remember the day she

died?"

"Very well. It was Edgar's birthday."

"Who's Edgar?"

"My husband, God rest his soul."

Dale nodded. "Do you remember seeing Ms. Metcalf coming or going that day?"

"Do you think she killed her? I knew it. I knew there was something wrong with that woman."

"I don't think anything either way. I'm just trying to get the facts."

Phyllis stared at him sideways. After a sigh, she continued. "It was about one or one thirty or so. She bolted out the door and burned rubber down the street. You can probably still see the skid marks right over there." She pointed across the street.

"A.M. or P.M.?"

"A.M."

"Did you see her coming or going any other time that day?"

"No, but she keeps her car or truck or whatever those SUV things are in the garage. I might have missed her leaving earlier and coming back. What time was Mrs. Arbeson killed?" Phyllis tilted her head and crossed her arms.

"I can't say, Mrs. Watcomb. I'm just trying to put together a sequence of events."

"Not much good then, are you?"

"I'm afraid not." Dale smiled and turned. *The world's full of them*, he thought.

Julia Metcalf's alibi had some holes. The kid, on the other hand, had a solid alibi. Dale's gut told him that Julia was innocent, and that Seth was involved. Possibly on the fringe, but in it up to his scrawny neck.

CHAPTER TWENTY-THREE

IT WAS 2:00 A.M. WHO WOULD BE knocking on her door at that hour? Slowly she crept through the kitchen.

"Who's there?" she asked as she laid a hand on the butcher knife.

"It's Tony."

Letting out a sigh, she unlocked the back door and reset the alarm. He slid his arms around her and kissed her. She looked incredibly sexy in the oversized shirt she'd been sleeping in. Her long legs were bare and the shirt was enticingly low cut.

She felt him tighten his embrace, and she kissed his neck. "It seems so long since I saw you last."

"Too long. I can't stay away from you, Jule." He kissed her hair and ran his hands up her back, shoulders, and neck then took her face in his hands and kissed her longingly.

Her response was of aching desire. Her lips softened and parted. His tongue slowly worked hers, sending sparks through her body. His hands roamed up her back. A sexy moan escaped her. Julia turned toward the stairs, leading him to her bedroom.

Once upstairs, he stripped off her shirt and began caressing her body. Her head dropped back and her eyes closed as she relished the sweet sensation.

After a moment, she began unbuttoning his shirt. She wanted to feel his bare chest against hers. Her hands began to tremble as she unfastened his jeans and ran her hands over his butt then drew him close. Everywhere her flesh met his tingled with longing.

His clothes dropped to the floor and he edged her close to the bed, still kissing and tasting as they moved. She sat on the edge and pulled him with her.

She ran her fingers through his hair and moaned softly as he worked his way south. Her movements became frantic. She arched and shuddered, crying out his name. He could hardly hold himself back.

She smiled and stretched. "Mmmm..." she murmured as she slid her arms around him.

"You look quite satisfied."

"You think?"

"I'm not done with you yet."

Her smile broadened. "Gee, I hate when that happens."

After being completely and thoroughly satisfied they lay looking into each other's eyes.

Tony kissed her hand. "How did your session with Dr. Ingvaldson go?"

Julia looked away. "It's painful to remember, let alone talk about."

"You can tell me when you're ready. It doesn't have to be now." He stroked her cheek.

"It's just that I can't be sure what parts were real, and which were symbolic. It was very violent, and graphic."

Tony pulled her close. "Shh. Just rest." He stroked her

back until she fell asleep.

ONCE AGAIN, JUST BEFORE dawn, Tony slid out of Julia's bed and began to dress.

"Are you leaving?"

"I have to, Jule. We'll have to be more careful, and I can't stay over again until this is over."

She propped up on one elbow. "But you're here now."

He smiled sheepishly. "I didn't intend to stay more than a few minutes."

"Then why did you come?"

"To give you this." He reached into his jacket pocket and handed her a disposable cell phone. "What it lacks in technology, it makes up for in anonymity. It can't be traced."

She took the phone and looked it over.

"What if we meet somewhere?" She sat up. A look of profound sadness spread across her face.

"Like where? I'm sure they will be keeping tabs on us. I would if it were me."

She smiled. "Then we'll be not-so-obvious."

He ran a hand down her cheek.

"Are you a church going man, Tony?"

"For you, I could become one."

"How about the basement of St. Ann's Church? We can arrive separately and sneak in the back way, near the rectory."

He looked at her, puzzled. "What about the priest?"

"Father Paul is a dear friend."

Knowing there could be no intimacy, he was a little disappointed. But he reasoned, it would be worth it just to see her and hold her. Besides, he could refuse her nothing now. "Every Tuesday, 9:00 a.m.?"

She smiled. "I'll be there."

CHAPTER TWENTY-FOUR

DALE RUBBED THE FRINGE OF STUBBLE on his head and stroked his graying beard. He turned his laptop back on and stabbed at the keys as he signed on. *It's got to be here,* he thought. *There's got to be something.*

Among the items found at the scene were several unidentified fibers. The report from forensics labeled them as "possible polar fleece." They didn't match anything that the victim was wearing, but could have come from the victim's bedroom. Dale checked the inventory of items taken from the mansion. No polar fleece. *It could be from glove linings,* he thought.

His laptop beeped as his email received an incoming message. He read it, then jumped to his feet, and pulled on his jacket. His eyes never left the screen. He clicked on the PRINT command.

Forensics had identified the DNA found under Mae's fingernails. The DNA matched Lonny Beck. Six feet, five inches of stupid, with a long criminal history. He weighed in at roughly 300 pounds, and was reputed to have killed a man with his bare hands, but it was never proven. Known association with Albert Cordell. Dale whistled through his teeth.

Cordell was suspected of a great many crimes, but never convicted. He covered himself exceedingly well, and it was likely that the time Beck had done had been in Cordell's stead. It seemed Albert had an unending supply of scapegoats and attorneys.

Beck's address was a flop downtown. Dale picked his way through the debris in the alleyway and found a way into the condemned building. The odor of rotted food, rodents, and unwashed humanity hit him like a brick. He suppressed a gag.

The few remaining squatters knew nothing of Lonny Beck. Dale contacted Beck's parole officer, and was informed that at last report, Beck was presumed to have taken up residence with Cordell. Dale sniffed at himself and fervently wished he'd called the officer first.

Cordell's gated estate, Nevermore, boasted 118 acres, complete with his own stocked lake and golf course, not far from the Arbeson property. The grounds were surrounded by a stone wall, eight feet tall, with an elaborate gate that stretched across a spacious tree-lined drive. The whole set up screamed, "Get the hell out of here and don't come back." The house itself was a full quarter mile from the gate, with every security measure available.

Dale stood at the gate with his hands in his pockets, sizing up the cameras and sensors guarding it. He let out a low whistle and tossed the remains of his toothpick then pushed the CALL button and pulled another toothpick from his pocket.

Just one Marlboro, he thought, as visions of a bluish wreath of smoke entered his head. *That's all I want.*

"Yes?" the voice in the call box demanded.

"I need to talk to Lonny Beck."

"This is the home of Albert Cordell."

"No kidding. My name is Detective Sergeant Dale Melhus. I need to talk to Lonny Beck."

A short silence followed. "This is the home of Albert Cordell," the voice repeated.

Dale sighed. "Okay, I need to talk to Mr. Cordell."

"Whom shall I say is calling?"

Dale gritted his teeth. "Detective Sergeant Dale Melhus."

"To what does this pertain?"

None of your damn business, Dale thought. "I'll discuss that with Mr. Cordell."

"I'm afraid Mr. Cordell is unavailable at this time."

Dale ran a hand over his face and mentally counted to ten. "Tell Mr. Cordell to make himself available, or I will take him to the precinct as a material witness, and quite possibly forget he's there."

The gate slowly opened, and Dale got back into his car and drove it down the wide tree-lined drive. He parked in front of the door where the butler was waiting.

"Was that you I was talking to out there?" Dale asked, pointing his toothpick at the slight man.

The butler sniffed and wrinkled his nose. Dale casually put his hands in his pockets and stared calmly at the butler, who stood stock-still.

"Announce me, Jeeves, or I'll announce myself."

The butler stiffened, turned on his heel, and stalked off down the hall. Dale followed him in. The interior appeared even larger than the exterior, which was formidable. Dale whistled through his teeth and removed his toothpick. Footsteps sounded down the hallway as Dale stuck the toothpick in his jacket pocket and waited.

ALBERT CORDELL STOOD BEFORE the mirror perfecting the curl in his mustache.

"Sir?"

"Yes, Milbert?"

"There's a detective downstairs who demands to speak with you. I tried to dissuade him, but he is quite insistent."

"Very well."

Milbert Hennings had become known to Cordell through his "family" connections. After several successful assignments, Cordell realized that it was more advantageous to keep a man with Hennings' temperament and skills close at hand, and happy. All he required was a word or two of praise occasionally, along with a challenging assignment to keep his blood lust under control. With Hennings, all play and no work had bitter consequences. When he was upset, the performance of the household staff declined greatly. And that was a disappointment to Albert.

One never wanted to disappoint Albert Cordell. The consequences were too dire. It was of no concern to Cordell if the upstairs maid's husband never came home. Or the groundskeeper had an accident resulting in his losing an ear. The mere appearance of disloyalty put the staff and their loved ones in peril.

Milbert was the only one who had needed no coercion to gain his loyalty. He and Albert were kindred spirits with their black hearts and mercenary intentions. Each might have considered the other a brother, had they possessed any human emotion.

Lonny was another story. He was intensely loyal as well, but with his diminished capacity and volatile temper, one could never tell when he might turn.

Lon had been assigned to Cordell many years prior by higher-ranking people in the organization. Albert thought the choice a poor one. Lon had to be told several times what his duties were and how they were to be carried out. Cordell's patience had nearly worn through when one night, shortly after Lon was assigned to him, a colleague assigned to make deliveries from Cordell to his superiors broke into the modest house that Cordell owned at the time. The man had come to assassinate him.

"Good evening, Al." The man sneered; the pistol in his hand never wavered.

"I prefer Albert."

"I'll just bet you do."

"To what do I owe this pleasant little visit?" Albert tried to kill enough time to figure a way to stop the man.

"It appears you've pissed someone off. Gotta tell you, I've never really liked you. It'll be my pleasure to off you."

"And what is my alleged transgression?"

The man chuckled. "That's the beautiful part. That package I was supposed to deliver to the bosses for you? I kept it for myself and told them you didn't have the money." His grin widened to expose his tar-stained teeth. Albert was repulsed by the sight of it, imagining the sickening odor that must have accompanied it.

"So I am to die for your crime?"

The man laughed and stretched the pistol toward Cordell. "Goodbye, Al."

The sound was deafening as the gun went off. A large shadow crossed the room at that moment and landed with a thud at Cordell's feet. A feral noise began to emanate from the giant on the floor. Neither Cordell nor the man sent to shoot him could do anything but stare as the behemoth straightened up holding his shoulder. He strode toward the assassin and picked him up by the neck as though he weighed nothing. Lonny flung the man across the room. A second later, he had the man in his grasp once more and began to pummel *him mercilessly.*

Albert watched in awe. A couple minutes later, it was obvious the man was not getting up ever again.

"Lon," Cordell said, but there was no response. "Lon!" Cordell shouted.

Lonny's head snapped around as he was about to deliver another blow.

"He's dead. You need medical attention. Stop hitting him."

Lon's breath was like a freight train. He stopped and looked at the assassin with his fist still cocked. Then he looked at his shoulder and saw the blood flowing down his arm. He dropped the assassin and started to cry like a child.

"There now, Lon. I'll fetch someone to tend to your wounds. Then you can take this... this thing to the woods. I don't want him found, Lon. Do you understand?"

"Yes, Mr.Cordell," Lon managed between sobs.

That day, Albert's respect for Lon increased one hundred fold.

Albert Cordell strode into the foyer and stopped several feet from Dale. His gait was graceful and careful, as though he were gliding.

"Officer, ahh...?" He glanced at the card proffered by Dale and pinched it between his slender fingers as though it were filthy. "Melhus. How can I help?"

The butler took the card as Albert wiped his hands on a handkerchief. He folded them neatly in front of him, awaiting Dale's reply.

Dale looked him over. *There's a grown up case of child abuse if I ever saw one,* he thought. He stuck out his hand. "It's Detective, like I told Jeeves, here."

Albert tilted his balding head and stared at Dale's outstretched hand a moment. His dark, thin hair was intricately swirled on his shining head, and his mustache was waxed into tiny loops above the corners of his thin, stern-looking lips.

Melhus' eyebrows rose as he stared at Cordell's distinctive swirled hairdo. Cordell turned his gaze back to Dale's face.

"His name is Milbert."

Dale nodded. "I have a few questions for you, Mr. Cordell, and it may take several minutes. Might you be more comfortable if we sit down?"

"No."

"All right. I'm going to record our conversation, with your permission, which I'm sure will be no problem, since you have nothing to hide. Am I right?" He smirked as he dug in his jacket pocket.

"I may choose not to answer." Cordell raised his chin defiantly.

"Right." Dale took a toothpick from his pocket and slid it into his mouth. He fiddled with the pocket recorder and took a step closer to Cordell.

Immediately, Albert backed away, as though Dale were infectious. Melhus stopped and a slight smile played across his face. "Do you have a man named Lonny Beck in your employ?"

"Yes."

"Is he here?"

"No."

"Do you know where he is?"

"No."

"Chatty, aren't you?"

Cordell looked at Dale with disgust. "Are you quite finished, Officer?"

Dale sighed and twirled his toothpick before taking it from his mouth and pointing it at Cordell. "It's Detective, and no, I'm not."

The interview continued in kind for the better part of the

afternoon. At last, Dale wrapped it up.

Still standing stock-still, Albert Cordell carefully dabbed small beads of perspiration that had formed on and around his waxed and curled mustache. Milbert had stood at his side fetching him water when he needed it, but offering nothing to Dale.

"Look." Melhus' voice had gone thin with exasperation. "I'd hate to have to drag you to the precinct with me, Mr. Cordell. Lying about Lonny Beck's whereabouts will land you in a cell."

Albert Cordell looked slightly concerned. "I'll make you a deal, Officer. I will attempt to locate Mr. Beck, and make arrangements for you to speak with him."

Dale nodded and plopped down on a delicate antique settee placed near the entryway. "It's Detective. And I'll wait right here."

Cordell's anger flashed in his eyes, and they seemed to burn holes in Dale. He threw an arm over the back of the settee and crossed his legs.

Cordell leaned toward Milbert and whispered softly. He then turned and walked off. Milbert turned his attention to Dale.

"Mr. Cordell is finished with this interview. You are to leave, or a formal complaint will be filed." The scrawny man stood silently, looking down his nose at Dale.

He slowly got up from the settee and looked Milbert in the eye. "Harboring a fugitive is a serious offense, Jeeves. You keep that in mind. Oh, and one more question? How long does it take him to swirl his hair like that? I'll bet it's longer than my ex-wife, and let me tell you, that's a considerable amount of time."

Dale smiled and let himself out. He sat behind the wheel of his car for a moment and looked around. He needed a better feel for the place, and its owner. After a moment he got out and leaned up against the fender of his unmarked unit. His gaze tracked over as much of the terrain as he could take in.

After a moment, the door to the house opened, and Milbert reappeared. His arms were crossed as he stared impatiently at Dale. "I've been instructed to file a complaint, Officer."

Dale smirked and tossed his toothpick to the ground. "Car won't start. The tow truck is on its way," he lied. "City doesn't spend much on maintenance." With one ankle crossed over the other he resumed his visual scan of the house and grounds.

"You will be off of this property in thirty seconds, or your superior will be notified."

"Can you give me a jump? That would probably be the fastest way to get me and my unit off the property." He leaned into his car and popped the hood.

Milbert disappeared. Dale used the opportunity to call in to the dispatcher and advise her of his location and status.

Moments later, a short, stocky man trudged from behind the mansion with a jump box in his hand. He hooked it up to Dale's car wordlessly. When the cables were secure he stepped back.

"You can try it now," he said.

Dale noticed that a chunk of the man's right ear was missing. He ducked into the car and turned the key. He was thankful the man hadn't tried the ignition himself, or his lie would've been discovered.

"Thanks," Dale said as the man unhooked the cables.

He merely nodded as he walked away.

"Hey, wait a sec," Dale called after him.

He shook his head and kept moving. Dale trotted over to catch up.

"Wait a sec, fella."

The man glanced up at the mansion and then turned to

Dale.

"Please, Mister. Just go."

The terror on his face Dale stopped in his tracks. He watched him walk away for a moment, and then turned back to his car.

CHAPTER TWENTY-FIVE

THROUGH THE SMALL BASEMENT WINDOW, JULIA watched Tony's borrowed car pass the church three times before he parked in the lot and sneaked in the back door.

She didn't hear him slip quietly down the stairs to the church basement, but knew that he would find his way. He apparently didn't see her lurking behind the dishwashing station in the kitchen.

"Julia," he whispered. She stepped out, his embrace enveloped her like a warm cozy blanket, and their lips touched tenderly.

"Why do we have to hide like we're doing something wrong?"

"It's just until the investigation is over. The defense will use our relationship to cast doubt, and make it look like we are trying to deflect charges to someone beside you. It's taken less than that to throw an entire case. We're lucky that you know and trust the priest here."

"He was Mae's brother's best friend. After Eddie

drowned, Paul and I became friends. At first, he was angry with me for dreaming about it, but in time he realized there was nothing I could have done to save poor Eddie." She looked away wistfully. "He's been my big brother since then, always watching out for me. I haven't told him anything about us yet. He knows I will when I'm ready. I wanted to run it past you first."

"The way he was eying me, I think you should. I have a strict policy never to piss off the clergy. They have friends in really high places."

She laughed. "You're right. I'll sit down with him next week and catch him up."

"I tried to get Melhus to tell me about the case," Tony said.

"And?"

"He won't tell me much. That's good, I guess. That way I can't be accused of influencing the case."

"I still hate sneaking around."

"Me too. Believe me, I'd love to parade around with you on my arm."

A smile spread across her face. "When was the last time you paraded?"

He chuckled softly. "I brought this for you, Jule." He pulled a pretty gift box out of the bag he carried in with him and handed it to her.

Wordlessly, she looked at him and took the box. She untied the silky red ribbon and let it float to the floor. When she looked inside the box, she began to laugh.

"Do you like it?" He asked.

"I love it." She pulled the dream catcher out of the box and held it up. The colored crystals fastened into the web of string danced in the light. Instead of the traditional feathers, it trailed ribbons bejeweled with more crystals and beads.

"I'll hang it over my bed to catch all the bad ones." She

leaned over and kissed him. "Thank you, it's beautiful."

"I love seeing you smile. There's been too much pain in your life."

"I'm getting better. You're a big part of that." She put her hand on his.

He circled her waist with his arms and kissed her deeply, holding her close. Emotion choked her, and she backed away.

"Are you okay?" he asked.

"I'm fine. It just seems awkward to be feeling the way I do right now in church."

He turned her loose, but hung on to her hand. "I have to go, Jule." He kissed her hand and then her cheek. "Go straight home, and lock your door. I'll talk to you soon."

He took the stairs two at a time. His long look around told him it was safe, before he went out to the lot and his borrowed car.

CHAPTER TWENTY-SIX

"MILBERT," CORDELL SNAPPED. "THIS IS BECOMING cumbersome."

"Yes sir."

"Go get that insipid child. We'll keep him here where we can control his movements."

"Yes, Mr. Cordell."

"Does he really think I would just forget that he is indebted to me?"

"No, I'm sure not."

"And what of the Metcalf woman? It's not her money. It should have gone to the boy. Then his debt would be paid." Cordell stared at Hennings.

"You're right, Mr. Cordell."

"Get me the boy and the woman."

"And the police officer who treated you so disrespectfully?"

Cordell eyed Hennings for a moment. "You may do as you wish with him."

Hennings smiled broadly. "Thank you, Sir."

"It doesn't come back to me. Am I clear?"

"Yes, Sir."

"Off with you."

Hennings unlocked the storage building at the rear of the estate. As the door swung open, he drew in a breath, the substantial weapons collection arousing him. He selected a Remington 700 sniper's rifle. He hefted the weapon, checking its balance. The snick of the bolt action sent a pleasant shiver up his spine. Carefully, he positioned the stock against his shoulder and sighted in a tree several hundred yards away. Slowly, he lowered the rifle and ran a hand lovingly down the stock and over the barrel.

Hennings placed the rifle in a cleaning stand and began to disassemble it methodically. "A clean weapon is an accurate weapon..." he remembered.

His mentor's voice always entered his thoughts when he had a firearm in his hands. The Major was demanding and expected nothing less than perfection. He hand-picked Hennings after his tour in south-east Asia came to an abrupt halt. He wasn't supposed to get caught. But it was a helluva shot. The Army was sent to break him out of the Cambodian prison, but then they busted him down to Sergeant and chose not to accept his re-enlistment once he got stateside. That's when he met the Major and his band of mercenaries.

"So Hennings, tell me about your best shot," the Major demanded at their first meeting.

Hennings stood at parade rest. "Sir. My best shot was from a tree. About a thousand yards, sir, using an Army M21. I mortally wounded the target. I caught him in the gut, sir. He was a Cambodian General."

The Major laughed. "That was your best? When I'm finished with you, you'll double that range, and be able to take out your target in a goddamn tornado."

Hennings made the mistake of making eye contact with

the Major, not believing what he heard. That cost him a twenty-five mile run while he wore a full field pack and carried his rifle high over his head. Each time Hennings tired and began to lower his arms, the Major would shoot at Hennings' feet. He never again made the mistake of looking the Major in the eye.

Most of the jobs completed by Hennings were black ops, contracted by federal agencies. He travelled the world taking out those who stood in the way of truth, justice, and the American way. There were no records of these contracts or of the payments made to the Major and Hennings.

The Major never showed pride or admiration in his student. Instead, he constantly pushed for more. Less than absolute perfection was failure. If Hennings took out a target with anything but a head shot or a heart shot, the Major would literally train him until he lost consciousness. It varied as to whether his punishment was to run many miles with his weapon and a full field pack, traverse the obstacle course over and over, do pushups in a deep muddy puddle, or a combination of all of them.

The head shot was used strictly for execution. Equidistant between the eyes was preferred and expected. The heart shot was personal. It was meant to indicate a vendetta.

That's where Hennings had hit the Major. Right through the heart. He'd made sure the encounter was close enough that the Major knew exactly who hit him. He already knew why.

Afterward, he sold his trade to the highest bidder. That was how he met Albert Cordell. After several years, he grew tired of the constant travel and brushes with the law. Mr. Cordell hired him to supervise security at Nevermore. But occasionally, he was able to scratch the itch.

The Remington was perfectly cleaned and oiled. Milbert partially assembled it and laid it carefully in the duffel bag with the other items he'd need.

Anticipating Mr. Cordell's permission to hit the detective, Milbert had stolen an ID badge from a janitor at the courthouse. He put it and a set of non-descript coveralls into the bag. Tomorrow promised to be a good day.

Today, he would only need the Walther that he carried all of his waking hours.

CHAPTER TWENTY-SEVEN

THE MERE THOUGHT OF TONY SET Julia's heart aflutter. His rugged looks appealed to her. His salt and pepper hair perpetually looked like he'd just come in from a windstorm and she loved the way the corners of his eyes crinkled and his lips disappeared under his mustache when he smiled. But it was his eyes that attracted her the most. They portrayed every emotion and twinkled when he grinned. She touched her flushed cheek, where his hand had been only a few minutes before.

Julia bit her lip thoughtfully. No one knew that she snuck out to meet Tony, and she'd been careful. No one had followed her, she was certain. She decided it was safe to make a quick stop at the farmer's market on her way home from the church and pick up some fresh vegetables and a colorful bouquet of flowers.

She squeezed and sniffed and inspected until her tote bag was full. Her eyes darted around occasionally, but nothing seemed amiss.

As she climbed the front stairs to her door, she sensed movement behind her, but it was too late. Someone touched her arm from behind. Fruit and vegetables flew as she swung around with her fist.

It was after she struck her assailant at full thrust that she realized it was Detective Melhus. Her hands flew to cover her open mouth as he landed flat on his behind at the bottom of the stoop.

"Oh, I'm so sorry!" she exclaimed. Her knuckles hurt so she shook her hand.

Dale rubbed the side of his face and he clambered to his feet. "That's a hell of a left hook you got there." He moved his jaw around and shook his head.

"Let me get you some ice," she said, unlocking her door. She hurried to the kitchen. In one smooth motion, a bag of frozen peas was out of the freezer and a towel neatly wrapped around it.

Dale picked up her groceries and followed her in. He placed the bag on the counter and sat at the dinette.

"Don't suppose you have a cigarette?" he asked.

"Sorry, I quit years ago."

He nodded and pulled a toothpick from his pocket as he pressed the bag of peas to the side of his face. Julia sat across from him not knowing what to say or do. She had just assaulted a police officer.

Her eyes couldn't meet his. After a long pause, she spoke. "I suppose you'll be arresting me." She stared at the floral print tablecloth and wrung her hands. Worry creased her brow.

Dale's laughter started somewhere below his gut and slowly erupted, gaining momentum like a volcano. After a moment, he was doubled over slapping the tabletop with his free hand.

Julia stared at him as though he were crazy.

"Oh that's rich, lady." The bubbling chortles precluded

any ability to speak further.

"Well, I hit you," she said, still puzzled by his reaction.

Tears rolled down Dale's face as he finally gained control. "Actually, I was really glad you did. I was worried about you, since you were oblivious to my presence. I followed you from the church."

Her gaze quickly shifted.

He studied her for a moment. "May I ask what you were doing at the church?"

Her stomach flipped as she quickly thought up a lie. "Well praying, of course. What do you do at church?" She crossed her arms defensively.

"Okay, but it's hard to help you when you're lying. You know that, right?"

"Why were you following me?"

"Actually, I was on my way here to ask you a few more questions about Seth. I happened to see you come out of the church, so I followed you."

"You might have let me know sooner."

Dale nodded. "I guess I could have, but I wanted to be sure I was the only one doing the following. I was."

She nodded. "What do you want to know about Seth?"

"Well, you control his trust fund, right?"

"Yes, that's right."

"Has he asked you to turn control over to him, or get him a distribution he doesn't have coming to him?"

"Well, he was really angry when he found out he didn't get control of the trust. He told me that I'd better do it his way. Then he said that Mae was stubborn at first. He intimated that he'd done something to make her more co-operative, but I took it as posturing since Mae never mentioned anything to me. Then he tried to convince me to get him a ten thousand dollar advance."

"Tried?"

"He told me he needed to pay his student loans. He hasn't any, so I told him no."

"What was his reaction?"

"He was royally perturbed, of course. I chalked it up to another of his outbursts."

Dale nodded. "Always a brat, huh?"

"Since the day he was born."

"He was at The Wherehouse Nightclub the night Mrs. Arbeson disappeared. We were able to verify his alibi and found any number of witnesses for whom he personally poured the Cristal from 10:00 until 12:30ish. The alarm company confirmed that the system was shut off at 9:30 and reset at 12:54. Young Mr. Arbeson says the help must have forgotten to set it when they left. Phone records indicate you called at 1:07. He didn't do it."

"I know that. He's a jerk, but he wouldn't murder Mae in cold blood."

"Do you think he might have hired it?"

Julia blinked several times. "I don't think so. I could see him having her kidnapped, but murdered?" She chewed a thumbnail and gave it a think.

Dale watched her a moment and decided he'd gotten all he could from her. He handed her the bag. "Thanks for the peas. Here's my card, in case you think of anything else."

"Wait, what about the floral delivery guy?" She shivered involuntarily at the memory.

"Developed a bad case of laryngitis. He won't even post bail. We can't get anything out of him."

She frowned. "What will happen to him?"

"He'll likely plead guilty and do his time."

"How much time?"

"That depends on his record and the judge. You don't need to worry. He'll be away for quite a while."

"He was hired, though. What about the ones who hired

him?"

"We'll have to find another way. Without his testimony, that angle won't work."

She nodded.

He hoisted himself up out of the chair and headed for the front door.

"By the way, Ms. Metcalf, when you go back to church? To pray? Say hi to Tony for me." He winked and let himself out.

CHAPTER TWENTY-EIGHT

RON LONGSTREET WAS A MOUNTAIN OF a man. His broad shoulders and trim waist made his six-foot-five-inch frame most imposing. Icy blue eyes were set deep between his high-and-tight military hair cut and chiseled cheekbones. He stood in the foyer of the Arbeson estate waiting to be announced. The pompous prick who now owned it kept him waiting. The longer he waited, the more he wanted to punch the little jerk right in the face.

Ron's controlled demeanor threatened to crack as Seth finally deigned to grace him with his presence. Seth's mouth fell open at the sight of Ron's football-player physique.

"Who are you and what do you want?" he demanded.

"Mr. Arbeson, I'm Ron Longstreet from the Blair Agency. Mr. Halberg hired me to investigate Mrs. Arbeson's death."

"Even Blair's offer of a million dollar reward hasn't turned up anything. What makes you so special?" The snide little jerk relaxed. That was a mistake.

The impact into the wall sent Seth's chewing gum sailing

over Ron's left shoulder and halfway across the entryway. His feet dangled several inches off the ground, and the wheezing noises he made told Ron that he'd hit the mark with his elbow.

By now the kid was probably feeling like his chest was going to implode. He had only knocked the wind out of him, but enough continued pressure on his ribs would make him feel like he was dying.

"Listen, you smart ass," Ron hissed. "You're gonna tell me everything. And I mean everything you know about this whole thing. And you're gonna do it now."

"Can't... breathe," Seth replied. His eyes watered and his tongue protruded from his open mouth as he tried to suck in air.

For effect, Ron let up the pressure and then reapplied it. "How about it? You ready now?"

"Okay," he wheezed.

Ron relaxed his grip, but continued to hold him in place.

Elsa rounded the corner and stopped dead. A small squeaking sound emanated from her lips and the blood drained from her face. Ron reached his free hand into his pocket and pulled out his credentials. He tossed them at her. "I work for Phineas Halberg."

"Oh, I... oh." Her mouth opened then closed.

He turned his attention back to Seth. "Talk."

"Well, um. I hired some guys to kidnap Mae."

Elsa gasped and started to sob.

"I mean, it was wrong. But she wouldn't give me control of my trust. That's all I was thinking of. They were just supposed to hold her overnight, and rough her up a little. Then I could go to Phin and get the ransom money. I never wanted her killed."

"Who did you talk to?"

"The big guy they sent to collect the money. I think they called him Lon."

"Lonny Beck? Thug."

"Yeah. I thought he was gonna break my thumbs. That Lon guy told me to leave the alarm disarmed and he'd take care of the rest. I had to sign some papers, too."

"What papers?"

"I don't know, something about control of the trust."

Ron looked at him unblinking. "Are you stupid?"

"Look, all I know is if I didn't sign, they'd make sure I couldn't ever sign anything again."

"And you trusted these people? I ask again, are you stupid?"

"I didn't have any choice, okay?" His voice rose with tension.

"They're coming back, you know."

"I've been keeping the system armed and I have a gun."

Ron nearly snickered. "What kind of gun?"

"It was Father's. A twenty-two something or other."

"Jesus, kid. Keep going. Who was supposed to call and demand ransom?"

"Lon and some smaller guy were the only ones I ever saw."

"The smaller guy — what did he look like?"

"I don't know. About my height maybe. Skinny, white. Little mustache."

Ron pulled out his cell phone and dialed. "Gimme Phin." He paused. "Phin, the kid's gonna need somebody here." He listened a moment. "No, he says he didn't have her killed. That he only contracted to extort a ransom. I believe him. But Lonny Beck is involved."

He hung up and turned back to Seth.

"Are you gonna call the police?"

"That's Phin's call. Somebody from Blair will be here in a couple of hours. Send home the servants, lock the door, and sit tight." Ron turned.

"You're gonna leave me here unprotected?"

Ron stopped and faced Seth. "What? The alarm system and your .22 suddenly quit working?"

"You can't..."

"I met your stepmother once. Yeah, I can."

CHAPTER TWENTY-NINE

"WHAT DO *YOU* WANT?"

Julia's fist was on her hip. At least Jeff had combed his hair.

"Well, can't a guy come and visit his favorite ex-wife?" He smiled.

"Not without some reason. Again, what do you want?"

"Well, okay. I'll get right to the point. Can I come in?"

"No."

"Geez, Jule. Don't be like that."

"Your point, Jeffrey?"

"Oh yeah. Um, I was thinking that now that you have all that money, that I should take you back to court for some alimony. Or, you could just give me a settlement and we'll call it good."

"You're joking."

"No, actually, I'm serious."

"Go ahead. Take me to court." She put her fist back on her hip and swung the door shut. His hiking boot stopped it from closing.

"I don't think you want me to do that."

Julia sighed. "Get off my porch and never darken my door again."

"That cop came to talk to me, Jule. I could tell him anything, and he'd believe me."

"Tell him whatever you want."

"I'll call him if I have to."

"Just out of morbid curiosity, what do you think you could tell him that he would believe?"

"For starters, your little weed habit."

She blinked at him. "You're the one with the habit, Jeff."

"That doesn't mean you don't have one. Or that I couldn't tell him that." Jeff leaned in and an evil half smile developed. "I could tell them that you and Mae had a fight."

"I've had enough of this conversation."

"You think on it, Jule. I know enough to make it work. I'm gonna come back and we'll talk about how much my settlement will be." He turned and started toward the curb.

"Jeff?"

He spun. "Yes?"

"Kiss my ass."

CHAPTER THIRTY

SOMEONE AT THE GATE BUZZED NON-STOP.

"Thank God. It's about damn time they got here." Seth buzzed the gate open, certain it was the bodyguard. One look out the window made him painfully aware of the mistake he'd just made.

"Elsa, tell him I'm not here. Get rid of him."

"But Mr. Seth…"

"Do it now. Remember, I'm not here." Seth ran up the stairs.

Elsa opened the door.

"My dear lady. I wish to see Seth Arbeson. The matter is urgent. I will not be turned away."

The hair on the back of her neck stood on end. She knew that staying on until Seth found another housekeeper had been a mistake.

"I'm sorry, Mister?" She hoped she was smiling pleasantly.

"Hennings, Milbert." He smiled, tried to be charming. She

found it all the more disconcerting.

She told the trim and elegantly dressed man what Seth told her to say.

"I'm very sorry, Mister Hennings. I don't expect Master Arbeson home for some time. I'd be happy to give him a message for you."

"I'll wait," he sneered as he pushed past Elsa and made himself comfortable in the sitting room. "I'd like some coffee while I wait. Fresh brewed, with just a touch of honey. I don't suppose you have any fresh cream?"

"Yes sir." She scurried to the kitchen. It took all of her concentration to measure out the water and coffee grounds. Her shaky hands nearly dropped the carafe when Seth came down the back stairs.

"Well?"

"He's still out there," she whispered.

"Why didn't you get rid of him?" Seth's voice was low, but his anger level was high.

"He pushed his way in."

"Goddammit, Elsa. I asked you to do one simple thing." He pointed a finger at her face.

Her eyes narrowed. "I have had enough," she whispered. "I quit!"

"Wait, you promised."

"You don't care about promises, why should I?" She gathered up her purse and her sweater and nearly ran out the back door.

Seth swallowed hard. His jacket was in the front closet, and in its pocket were his wallet and keys. He leaned up against the counter and wondered how he could get past the sitting room and make a hasty exit.

"Ah, there you are."

The soft voice sent an icy chill up Seth's back. He slowly turned to find Milbert standing before him. At least it wasn't the big guy. For a moment, Seth thought he could take him. Then he saw the pistol gripped in Milbert's hand, and his lips curled into an evil smile. "Mr. Cordell requests the honor of your presence. Right now."

CHAPTER THIRTY-ONE

DALE FINISHED HIS SEARCH. CORDELL CAME up, but not Hennings. *Why?* The guy clearly had known association with Cordell. No record, no history, nothing.

His message notification beeped for the third time. He sighed and stabbed at his phone.

"Um, yeah, This is Jeff Metcalf. I, um… you said to call if I thought of anything else. And um… I thought you should know that Julia, um… she grows pot in her back yard, and ah… she said stuff about Mae last week. Mean stuff. Yeah. Isn't there some kinda reward or something? I heard that on the TV. Yeah, okay. Call me back, dude."

Dale's mouth curved upward as he listened. *This guy is way more stupid than I thought.*

He dialed Jeffrey Metcalf's number.

"Yeah?"

"Jeffrey Metcalf?"

"Um, no. He's not here."

"Jeff, it's Detective Melhus. You left me a message."

"Oh yeah. Right. The TV said something about a reward?"

"That's being offered by a private party, but I can pass your information along to the Blair Agency for you."

"Dude, that would be cool. Do you want my address so they know where to send the money?"

Dale chuckled quietly. *What an idiot.* "I have that information. I was at your house, remember?"

"Oh yeah, right."

"You understand that Ms. Metcalf would have to be convicted to collect, right?"

"Well, how long will that take?"

"I don't know. Could be months, or even years."

"Oh."

"One more thing."

"Yeah?"

"You'll have to testify to the things you left on my voicemail."

"I will?"

"Yes, so be very careful that you can prove your accusations."

"I have to prove it?"

"You ex-wife is innocent until proven guilty."

"Huh."

"I am obligated to tell you that the penalty for purgery will land you in jail. But you don't have to worry about that, do you, Jeffrey? I mean, you'd never lie to the police, would you?"

"I ah…"

"You call me back when you're ready to come in and give your sworn statement and turn over your evidence against Ms. Metcalf. Then I'll run it right over to the grand jury. Your ex-wife will probably be arrested the same day. That'll be the fastest way to get the reward."

"Um, okay."

"I'll be waiting here for your call."

"Yeah, bye."

The dejected tone in Jeffrey's voice made Dale want to laugh. Alternately, he felt sorry for Julia. Now everybody and their brother would have their hand out in her direction.

CHAPTER THIRTY-TWO

STILL NO ANSWER. JULIA'S FRUSTRATION HAD reached its limit. *Where could that stupid kid be?* He was supposed to meet her so they could discuss his trust disbursement. She'd decided to incrementally increase his allotment solely based on how it was spent. If he was responsible, the allotment would go up quarterly. If not, it would remain as it was. Julia hoped it would give him some incentive to tend to his own finances. She really hated being the big bad financial witch.

"More coffee?" Lois asked.

"No. I'm going over there and find the little twerp. Then I'm going to wring his neck. But not before I tell him what he's missing out on." She got to her feet and gathered her things.

"Shall I hold these papers?"

"I don't know. I'll call you, Lois."

She left Lois's office and headed out the door.

WHEN SHE ARRIVED AT the Arbeson estate, the front door stood wide open. Slowly, Julia tiptoed inside.

"Hello?" she called. "Elsa?" The sound echoed and a shiver ran up her back.

She called 911.

Dale arrived with the black and whites minutes later. "Well, Ms. Metcalf. What are you doing here?"

"I had a meeting with Seth and he didn't show up. I got mad and came over here to wring his neck, but when I arrived, the front door was standing open."

"Have you looked around? Is anything disturbed?"

"No, I stayed right here after I called."

"Okay, I'm going to walk you around. I don't want you to touch anything. Just tell me if anything is out of place or missing."

They walked through the sitting room, the music room, and the conference room. All was well. In the kitchen, the coffee maker sputtered and dripped fragrant brown liquid over the countertop and onto the floor. Whoever made coffee had not put the carafe under the spout. Julia rushed to shut it off, but Dale pulled her back.

"Don't touch it."

"But..."

"What part of 'don't touch anything' do you not understand?"

She nodded but continued to stare at the mess.

"Ms. Metcalf, the purpose of this little tour is to see what's out of place. I can already guess that the coffee all over the place is, so let's move on. I need your focus now."

They walked outside. "I don't see Elsa's car anywhere," Julia remarked.

"Didn't she inherit a million dollars?"

"Yes."

"Why would she still be here?"

"She agreed to stay on until Seth found a suitable replacement."

"Why?"

"She's a soft touch."

"She's a pushover."

"That, too. Can I call her? Just to make sure she's okay?"

"Yeah."

Julia took out both cell phones, and put the disposable back in her purse. Dale's eyebrows shot up, but he said nothing. Elsa answered on the first ring.

"Miss Julia," she exclaimed.

"Elsa, I'm at the estate. Why aren't you here? Did you find a housekeeper already?"

Elsa began to cry. "Oh Miss Julia, a man came to the door. A scary man. I lied and told him Master Seth wasn't home, but he pushed his way in..."

"Slow down, Elsa. You're not making any sense."

"Staying with him until the Blair Agency person got there was a mistake."

"Where is she?" Dale interjected. "I need to interview her. Now."

Julia shot him a glance. "Are you at home?"

"Yes, but I'm frightened, and I'm packing my things."

"Wait right there, I'm bringing the police. We're on the way." She snapped the phone closed and turned her attention to Dale. "Come on, she's scared and she may leave."

They ran to Dale's car. He slammed it into gear and picked up the radio. He had dispatch send a car to Elsa's to stand guard.

MOMENTS LATER, THEY WERE in Elsa's living room trying to

calm the hysterical woman.

"I have to leave," she said.

Julia slipped into the kitchen and brewed a cup of herbal tea. Elsa's hands shook violently as she accepted the cup that Julia prepared for her.

"Ma'am, Seth wasn't at the house when we arrived, and Julia says the front door was standing open. Does that seem normal?"

Tears welled in Elsa's eyes. "Mr. Seth would never have left the door open." She shot a look to Julia. "Was his car still there?"

"Yes."

"Oh, no." Elsa set down her cup and buried her face in her hands. "Mr. Seth isn't the best boss anyone could ask for, but I've known him since he was a baby." She looked imploringly at Dale. "Please don't let anything happen to him."

"We'll do our best, Ma'am. What time did you leave the estate?"

Elsa sniffed and sat up straighter. She gripped Julia's hand for a moment before answering. "About two hours ago."

Dale nodded. "You mentioned a man who came to the door. What did he want?"

"Um, let me think." Her brow wrinkled in concentration. "He said he needed to talk to Mr. Seth. He said it was urgent, and he, um…" She paused and thought a moment. "He said he wouldn't be turned away. Yes, that was how he said it." She smiled nervously and nodded.

"Very good. Now, can you describe him?"

"All I can tell you is that he made the back of my neck tingle."

"I'm sure you were very frightened. I would've been." Dale smiled as he tried to put her at ease.

"I can't remember what he looked like."

"Would you stand up a minute, Elsa?" Dale stood in front

of her. "Was he taller than me, or shorter?"

"Shorter. In fact I think he was just a bit taller than me. Not a very big fellow." Her brow furrowed again, and she stared off as she sank back into her chair.

Dale sat too and waited for the image to re-form in her head.

After several long minutes, she spoke. "He was perhaps sixty, with thinning hair cut short. He was well built, like he worked out a lot. Maybe a boxer. He seemed light on his feet. His clothes were neatly pressed, and his pants sharply creased. His eyes were brown, and I think that's what scared me most. It was... it's hard to explain."

"Go with your gut. What's the first word that comes to mind when you remember his eyes?"

Elsa looked at Dale. "Hate."

Dale sat back. "Do you remember anything else?"

"Um... he wanted coffee. I went to the kitchen to brew some. It had to be fresh. He was quite insistent about that. With honey and fresh cream."

"Then what happened?"

"Mr. Seth yelled at me for letting the man into the house. As though I could stop him." She sniffed. "I quit then and there and walked right out. That was the last straw. Now I feel bad. Mr. Seth is missing. I wonder if that would have happened if I stuck around."

"If what I suspect is true, and you had stuck around, Elsa, you would probably be dead."

She gasped and paled. "What about Mr. Seth? Do you think they've killed him?"

"I'm gonna do my best not to let that happen. They need him for now, so I think he's okay for the moment." He shot a glance at Julia. She was in serious danger now.

Dale dug out his iPhone and ran his finger over it. After a moment he turned it to Elsa. "I'm going to scroll through some pictures. You tell me if you recognize the man, okay?"

He got up to sit next to Elsa. She put on her readers and stared at the phone. Dale started with photos of two cops that they used for control subjects. He scrolled through six more. Lonny Beck and Albert Cordell were among them.

"No, he's not in those pictures."

"You're sure?" Dale tried not to sound disappointed.

"Yes, positive."

"Okay. Where were you thinking of going, Elsa?" Dale asked.

"My sister's in Cleveland."

"Store the car and take the train. Pay cash for the ticket. Here's my card. Buy a disposable cell and use it to make your calls to any contacts here. I'll notify the local police precinct and ask them to do extra patrols at your sister's until we catch this guy."

Dale wrote down Elsa's sister's address and contact information.

Once they were back in Dale's car, he turned to Julia. "What about you? You need a bodyguard."

"Don't be silly, Detective. I have the security system on the house."

He smirked at her. "Now that they have Seth, you are the only piece of the puzzle missing. You need protection."

She regarded him seriously. "I won't give up my freedom, Detective."

CHAPTER THIRTY-THREE

FATHER PAUL AND JULIA SAT IN the dining room in the basement of the church enjoying a cup of coffee. Their relationship completely overlooked the fact that Paul was a priest. They could and did talk about everything, and in no uncertain terms.

"So, what's going on with you and this Tony fellow?"

Ever the big brother, she thought. His eyes told her he was suspicious of the situation and wasn't about to be used anymore as their refuge without full disclosure.

Julia smiled at him. "He's a policeman, Paul. A detective."

"Why all the cloak and dagger? He's married, isn't he?"

"No. We just need to keep a low profile until they solve Mae's murder."

"What the hell difference does that make? He's playing you, Julia. I won't have that." His voice rose more than a few decibels.

"You sure are suspicious for a priest. And why is it that you swear when you're around me?" She smiled, but he didn't return it.

"Don't change the subject, Jule. Answer the question."

"The prime suspect is Albert Cordell. His very expensive table of attorneys would use anything they could to deflect guilt from their client. It'll be too convenient for them to link the initial investigator and the heir to Mae's estate."

Paul whistled. "I've heard of Cordell. He's really bad news. They did that news program on him a year or two back. They said he was some big crime boss, but he'd never done time because someone else always took responsibility. Or the witnesses developed amnesia. Or died mysteriously."

"Our relationship could be played up to look like he was trying to protect me and blame Cordell. I have no alibi for the night Mae was killed, and I inherited most of her holdings. Not that I want them. It's been a nightmare. I just want Mae back." Tears started, and she couldn't hold them back.

Paul took her hand. "Me, too."

Julia brushed at her face impatiently and headed for the kitchen. "Come on, Father. Let's get you set up for that confirmation lunch."

Father Paul followed, but it was obvious that the subject was not closed.

"I'm still not happy with this whole situation. Maybe you should hire a bodyguard," Paul suggested.

She stopped and looked at him for a moment before answering. "Absolutely not. I don't want some goon following me around for the rest of my life."

"It would only be until Mae's killer is caught."

"No way. I might as well be the one in prison."

"Please think about it, Jule. I'm so worried for you." He took her hand, and looked imploringly into her eyes.

She sighed. She'd never seen the pleading expression before. "All right. I'll think about it."

JULIA WAVED TO PAUL and looked around the parking lot carefully. After Melhus followed her, she had resolved to be more vigilant. She rounded the back of the van parked next to her SUV and pushed the remote to unlock it, but didn't hear the familiar *click*. She stopped between the trucks and extended her arm and pushed the button again.

The remote fell to the ground as massive arms grabbed her from behind. A hand with a cloth in it covered her face. It smelled like some sort of chemical. Her head spun. She held her breath and stomped on the big man's foot.

"Try that again," he said, tightening his grip on her.

An involuntary squeal escaped her lips as the necessity to breathe won out over her will. The wooziness intensified. Darkness clouded her vision. She tried to shake her head but his grip was too tight. The elbow Julia tried to swing into his torso barely moved from her side. She hoped fervently that Paul had seen them from the church and had called the police. As she withered, the man hauled her up off her feet and tossed her into the back seat of her car like a rag doll.

She fought the dizziness and watched the big man turn to the driver's door. Suddenly, he crumpled and fell to the ground. The car door flew open, and Paul pulled her from the car. "Can you walk Jule?"

"I, ah..." Her head was spinning.

Paul lifted her up and over one shoulder. She jolted and pitched as he ran for the church. Her stomach twisted and convulsed. He pulled the heavy door open, ducked inside, and set Julia down gently on the cold floor. It felt good against her face. Paul turned to lock the door just as the big man reached it. Paul's hands shook, but the lock clicked into place just in time. It was then Julia realized he was carrying a large candlestick like those that decorated the altar in the chapel.

There was a single *thump* on the door and the sound of footsteps running away. Paul's fingers trembled. "I'm calling 911."

Julia's stomach revolted and her head throbbed. Paul gathered her up and rocked her in his arms. She wanted to tell him to stop moving, but only garbled vowels came out. She pushed away from him just before she vomited on the hard floor. Paul held her head. He was telling her something. "...police are on the way, and an ambulance," she heard.

Her arms and legs felt like lead. She finally opened her eyes with great effort. Paul's face filled her field of vision. He was crying. "Jesus, Jule."

She tried to smile. "You're going to hell for that."

"I figure He'll forgive me," Paul remarked as he pulled her close and hugged her fiercely.

"Go easy, I don't think I'm done being sick." The clammy, woozy feeling was better, but hadn't passed by a long shot.

A loud *knock* on the door startled them both. Paul jumped to his feet and let the police and first responders in. One of them put an oxygen mask on Julia's face and cracked open the valve on the oxygen tank. Her head was still spinning, but she was aware that Paul was relating the story to the police.

CHAPTER THIRTY-FOUR

DALE SAT IN HIS UNMARKED CAR just outside the gates of Nevermore. The sun shone brightly, and it was unseasonably warm. Next to him on the front seat was a small cooler of Cokes and a pastrami sandwich. He watched the gate for Lonny Beck, but he never showed.

Milbert appeared about midway through the shift. Dale had gotten out of his sedan to stretch his legs. He leaned against the front fender of his car, twirling his toothpick. "Jeeves," he said.

"Mr. Cordell strongly suggests you leave, immediately."

"Is that supposed to scare me?"

"You have no right to be here."

Dale pitched his toothpick. "Good thing I'm a cop. You won't have to call them."

Milbert clasped his hands together and raised his nose. "Your disrespect will be reported to Mr. Cordell." He turned and headed for the house.

"No, not that. Please Jeeves, I'm beggin' you." Dale

chuckled as Milbert disappeared from sight.

Several minutes later, a van pulled out of the gate. Dale's gut clenched, and he dove back into the front seat. He hadn't gotten a good look at the driver and wasn't sure if it was Beck. He made a swift U-turn and hurried after the vehicle.

The van neither exceeded the speed limit, nor broke any traffic laws. Dale pulled up behind it and hit the lights and siren anyway. The windows were heavily tinted, so Dale could hardly see that there was a driver, let alone who it was. He walked cautiously up to the driver's window with a hand close to his weapon. "Hands on the wheel where I can see them."

"Officer, you are treading on dangerous ground. I have done nothing illegal. You are bordering on harassment." Milbert's pinched features wore a look of disdain as he peered down his nose at Dale.

Dale saw another van pass them out of the corner of his eye, with Beck at the wheel. "Get that taillight fixed," he lied as he ran for his car.

Melhus jammed the car into drive and pulled away from the curb. Just then, Milbert pulled out, cutting him off.

"Oh you are so going to jail, Jeeves," Dale muttered as Milbert scraped the side of Dale's car. He kept going, lights and sirens screaming, and called the incident in to the dispatcher.

Beck weaved in and out of traffic, turning corners and running traffic lights. Dale struggled to keep up and not endanger pedestrians. At last he was able to gain some ground and was right behind the van. Backup was still a good ten minutes away, but Beck hadn't pulled over yet. *Come on, come on,* Dale thought as he drummed his fist on the wheel of his car.

Suddenly, Beck punched the gas and hit the Kia in front of him. The Kia was shoved into the truck in front of it, leaving it looking like an accordion.

"Shit," Dale said as he hurried to the Kia and the injured driver. The airbag had deployed, and the driver was bleeding and semiconscious.

Out of the corner of his eye, he saw the van turn at the next intersection and disappear.

It was then it occurred to Dale that Milbert matched the description given to him by Elsa.

CHAPTER THIRTY-FIVE

LONNY BECK'S ROOM WAS IN THE pool house behind the main residence at Nevermore with an intercom system so that Cordell could summon him at will. The big man stood before Albert looking down.

"You have failed me, Lon."

He began to raise his head. "I know, but..."

"Silence," Cordell shouted. "I have not finished. What have I repeatedly asked of you? Respect."

Lonny nodded and hung his head.

"I realize you are not very bright, but really, Lon. It can't possibly be so difficult to remember." Cordell paused. "You understand, don't you?" His voice softened as though chastising a child. "You must be punished."

The big man began to tremble and his eyes begged for mercy.

"I know Lon. I don't want this anymore than you do. But what would it say to my other employees? That failure is acceptable?"

Lon's entire body slumped, and he gritted his teeth, preparing himself for the punishment to come.

"Lon, look at me. I must see in your eyes that your punishment is accomplishing its intention."

The giant looked reluctantly into Cordell's emotionless stare as the sap landed its first excruciating blow. Cordell's eyes danced with cruel enjoyment.

Albert Cordell dabbed the perspiration from his forehead and upper lip, careful not to disturb his waxed and curled mustache. He checked his watch. Had it only been ten minutes?

Lonny Beck lay curled on the floor whimpering.

Cordell stared for a moment, almost able to envision his father's face in place of Beck's. He shook his head. "I didn't want to hurt you, Lon. You left me no choice. See to it that you don't disappoint me again."

He strode back to the residence toying with the sap in his pocket, whistling.

Upon entering, Milbert stopped him. "Mr. Cordell? Does Mr. Beck require medical attention?"

"See to his comfort, Milbert. He's really no more than a very large child."

"Yes, sir." Milbert retrieved his first aid kit and headed for the pool house. As he approached, he heard the sound of Lonny Beck sobbing. He sighed and kicked over a watering can to signal his arrival.

The crying abruptly stopped. Milbert pretended not to notice Beck wiping his face with his large hands.

"Lonny? Are you all right?"

"Uh, I guess." Beck held a protective arm across the ribs on his left side.

"Let me see those ribs."

Carefully, Lon lifted his shirt. Milbert drew in a sharp breath. The vivid purple welts screamed against the pale white flesh of Beck's torso. He put down the bag and began to rummage through it.

"Milbert, I didn't mean to disappoint Mr. Cordell again. You'll tell him I didn't mean it, right?"

"Yes, Lon, I'll tell him. Hold still now." He gently probed the welts. Lonny cringed. "Take these."

Milbert handed Lon two white tablets. The pills were fast acting and soon Lonny was comfortably numb and sleeping soundly. Milbert shook his head softly, taped up the big man's ribs, and left him to rest.

CHAPTER THIRTY-SIX

PAUL INSISTED THAT JULIA BE TAKEN to the emergency room. They administered oxygen and released her with the provision that she not be left alone for the next twenty-four hours.

Paul stayed with her, read to her, and brought her soup. He even walked her to the bathroom when necessary.

Julia felt her life had become a whirlpool. Nothing was as it should've been.

The following day, she sat trembling as she waited for Phineas Halberg. Paul accompanied her to his office.

"Really Ms. Metcalf," Phin began. "I must insist upon hiring a bodyguard. Father Paul will back me on this."

She narrowed her eyes at Paul. "I don't want some oversized gorilla following me around," she complained.

"You must have some protection. Attempts have been made to harm your person."

She sighed. "I know. But it's just not fair."

Paul patted her hand. "I know it's hard."

"We use the Blair Agency for such things. They're discreet

and reliable." Phin stood and paced the room.

"Discreet? Discreet doesn't get me any privacy. They'll be a part of every facet of my life. I'll never be able to shower, go to the bathroom, pluck a stray hair, or pig out on ice cream without someone knowing about it. What kind of life is that?"

"Ms. Metcalf…"

She straightened and looked Phin in the eye. "Would you like to live that way?"

He smiled patronizingly. "No, but please remember, it's only until they catch those who would do you harm."

"Which will be when?" She crossed her arms and shoved back the tears that threatened to flow.

Paul slowly shook his head. "I'm sorry, but I'm afraid it isn't up for discussion, Jule. And stop with the dirty looks. I'm a priest for crying out loud."

"I'll deal with you later." She pointed a finger at Paul and turned her attention back to Phin. "Can't I hire my own security?"

Phin's head swayed from side to side. "How well do you know another firm? We've used Blair for years. They've promised me their best."

She was silent for a moment. She looked at Paul and Phin in turn. They were right, and she knew it. "Fine."

"Done." Phin smiled and stuck his hand in Paul's direction. They shook hands.

He turned to his intercom. "Send in Mr. Longstreet."

Ron Longstreet looked every bit as Julia expected — large and imposing, with an icy stare. His blue eyes took in everything. His nose was slightly off, but rather than detract from his looks, it seemed to enhance them. He was dressed in a three-piece suit and carried himself like an athlete.

"Ms. Metcalf, it's very nice to meet you." He spoke in a monotone and his speech was clipped.

Her jaw dropped. She shook his hand and was amazed

by the gentleness with which he held hers.

Phin rubbed his hands together nervously. "Mr. Longstreet will need to stay with you at all times, Ms. Metcalf." He smiled expectantly.

"What?"

"I'm afraid I must insist."

"But I didn't think…"

"It's all right, ma'am. I can assure you that I am a professional, and my conduct will be as such during the length of my stay. Please sit. We have a lot to discuss." He smoothed his crisply creased trousers and unbuttoned his jacket revealing his weapon in its shoulder holster.

"I don't like guns in my house, Mr. Longstreet."

"I can't do my job without it," he replied.

Julia endured the interview with more patience than she had shown in a very long time. At its conclusion, she'd deduced that Ron was competent and would keep her safe, but on a personal level, he seemed a brute.

He followed her home, but would not allow her to even park in the garage. He stood at her car window. "Look," he said. "I have to check it out before you go in."

"I locked the door and set the alarm when I left. I'm pretty sure it's okay."

"Still, you can't go in until I check."

She sighed, handed him the key, and gave him the security code. Her eyes rolled as he drew his weapon before slipping quietly into the garage. The longer she waited, the angrier she became. She didn't need this big goon. Who did he think he was?

Her heart gave a little jolt when he appeared suddenly at her passenger window. "It's all clear," he said.

"I told you it would be."

He smirked. "Come on. We can't leave you out here. You might as well paint a big target on your head."

159

He followed her from room to room as she put away her things. After a few minutes of this, she'd had enough. "I'm going upstairs to shower. Alone."

"What do you mean?" His head tilted in puzzlement.

"You're following me everywhere and invading my personal space. I figure the shower is my only escape."

"Excuse me, but I'm only trying to do my job. Once I know your habits, I'll back off. But right now, this is the best way to protect you."

"Protect me from your own space. There's the den. The day bed is all yours." She stomped up the stairs and slammed the bathroom door.

The lavender scented bubbles floated her into a much more relaxed state. Suddenly, she heard a loud *thump*. *What now?* She sprang from the tub, sending bubbles flying everywhere.

She grabbed her robe and hurried down the stairs and through the swinging door to the kitchen. Ron knelt on the floor picking up a frozen roast that had fallen from the freezer.

"What are you doing?" she demanded.

"I was checking your freezer and this fell out."

"Put it back."

"Put it back? How? This freezer is a disaster. How can you live like this?"

Her fists went to her hips. "Put it back." Each word was punctuated with anger.

"Look, I'll just rearrange it a little, and everything will fit fine without breaking anyone's toes — namely mine — when you open it."

"No."

"But it's a mess."

"Maybe so, but it's my mess." She stalked over to where he stood and poked a finger into his chest. "Let's get this straight. This is my house. There's no reason to arrange anything that belongs to me."

"I have to know what, if anything, in this house is a potential weapon. When I come across anything that might be a danger to you, or me, such as falling frozen meat, it's my job to make sure that danger is neutralized."

"I hate you, Mr. Longstreet."

She turned and stomped off. Her head whipped around to glare at him when she heard his stifled snickers. A trail of bubbles led all the way back to the bathroom.

Julia called Tony on the disposable cell and told him about Ron.

"I'm going to check this guy out and call you back in a few," Tony said.

It wasn't long before her phone rang.

"He sounds like he's all right," he said. "I don't mind telling you I'm a little jealous of him."

She smiled. "There's no need to be jealous. He's a real pain in my butt."

"I checked his background. I'm impressed. He's been with Blair for over ten years. One of their best, from the look of it."

"He lurks around a lot."

Tony laughed. "I can't say I disapprove, or would do it any differently."

"It's creepy, and he keeps rearranging my stuff."

"You might as well get used to it."

"It puts a damper on my social life."

"Oh?"

"I can't sneak out and see my boyfriend." She smiled.

"Small price to pay. I'll bet your boyfriend will wait as long as it takes."

"I want to tell you about my session with Dr. Ingvaldson."

"Go."

"I don't want to talk about it over the phone. There are some details that might be helpful."

"Who are you talking to?" Ron asked as he appeared in her bedroom doorway.

Julia glared at him a moment. "Get out of my bedroom."

Ron scanned the room thoroughly and then turned his attention to look her in the eye. "It's my business to protect you. I need every piece of information I can get about you, the people you know, and your lifestyle if I'm going to do my job correctly. Now, who are you talking to?"

"None of your damn business," she said as she slammed the door in his face. She could hear Tony's laughter before she lifted the phone back to her ear.

"Not getting along with your new best friend?" he teased.

"He's driving me nuts. He may need a bodyguard of his own."

"Try to remember he's only doing his job."

"Yeah, right."

CHAPTER THIRTY-SEVEN

THE NEXT MORNING, JULIA WAS UP before dawn. Ron sat at the kitchen table. He appeared to be reading the paper, but his eyes left the page every few seconds to scan his surroundings. She smelled coffee. Good coffee. She gravitated to the cupboard to get a cup.

"Already poured you some. One cream, two sugar, right?"

"How did you know?"

"I'm a trained observer."

"Thanks." She sat down across from Ron and took a sip. It was perfect.

"Huh," he said.

"What?"

"I do believe that is the first time I've seen you smile."

Flustered, she looked away. "Well, don't get used to it."

"I'm going to ask you nicely, because I need to know. Will you please tell me who you were talking to last night?"

Her eyes narrowed, and she crossed her arms defensively. "My boyfriend," she said after some thought.

"Huh. Why all the secrecy?"

She was a bit shaken by his question. "I don't know what you mean."

"Really? Is he married or something?"

"No."

"Right. Let me make something clear to you. I can't protect you unless you are up front with me. You need to trust me. I don't really care what's going on with you and this guy. But I do need to know. Now spill it."

She debated for a moment. "He's my boyfriend. He's the cop who started the investigation into Mae Arbeson's death. We are keeping it on the down low until they catch the killers and put them away."

He cocked his head. "Are you sure this guy isn't married?"

CHAPTER THIRTY-EIGHT

ONCE AGAIN, DALE STOOD AT THE gates of Nevermore. "Open the gate. I have a warrant," he said when Milbert finally responded.

"What sort of warrant, Officer?"

"It's Detective, Jeeves. It's a warrant to search the premises. The entire premises if need be."

"Search for what?"

"Open the damn gate, Jeeves, or I'll arrest you myself for obstruction."

Several silent minutes passed. Dale turned to one of the uniforms standing nearby. "Get me the biggest vehicle we have here. We're gonna ram the gate. And find me a flippin' cigarette."

"Sure thing." The young officer smiled and disappeared.

Just then, a black limousine pulled up, weaving its way between the squad cars to the gate, and the window rolled down. The officer that the driver was speaking to pointed in Dale's direction.

"Betcha it's the lawyers," Dale said to no one in particular.

The limo pulled up next to Melhus. "Are you Detective Milhouse?"

"Close enough."

"I am Derrick Wilmington, Attorney for Mr. Cordell. I'll have a look at that warrant."

"Here, I made a copy just for you. Figured you'd join the party. You should know I plan to arrest the butler for obstruction. We've been standing out here for an hour."

"I know that isn't true, Detective."

Dale turned to the officer next to him. "How long have we been here, Smith?"

Smith looked at his watch and smirked at Dale. "About an hour, Detective."

Dale's toothpick twirled. "Get 'em to open the gate now."

The attorney pulled out his cell phone and dialed. Moments later, the gate opened and the parade of squads lined the wide drive. Halfway to the house, Dale spotted Lonny Beck walking toward them with his hands in the air.

"On your knees, Beck, hands behind your head," Dale barked. He had his pistol drawn and pointed at the huge man. Dale approached carefully and gestured for one of the uniforms to cuff him. He then patted Beck down and found him clean.

"Lonny Beck, you are under arrest for public endangerment, reckless driving, speeding, evading a police officer, leaving the scene of an accident resulting in injuries, attempted murder, and my personal favorite, the murder of Mae Arbeson. You have the right to remain silent..." He continued to recite the Miranda while two officers got Beck to his feet and placed him in the back of a squad.

"Well, Detective? The warrant was to search for Lonny Beck. You've found him. Now leave," the lawyer said.

"Not so fast. There's the matter of Milbert and the

obstruction charge."

"I'll bring him to the station."

Dale flicked the splinters of his last toothpick and stared the lawyer down for a moment. "All right. We are within our jurisdiction to search Lonny's room here."

"He is staying in the pool house. You will not be allowed into the main residence."

Dale's face tightened in frustration, but he said nothing. He was well acquainted with attorneys of this ilk and had learned the less said out loud, the better.

CHAPTER THIRTY-NINE

JULIA COULDN'T SHAKE THE FEELING THAT there was something in one of her journals that Mae had said in a dream. Something important, but she couldn't remember when. A year ago? Two? Ten?

Since Ron was holding her prisoner in her own home, she pulled several journals and began to skim them. After a lengthy search, she found it. Five years ago. She read it twice, just to be sure:

Mae and I skipped along the lakeshore. We were perhaps eight or nine years old. Splashing at the lapping waves, Mae suddenly stopped and waded over to me.

"Jule, wait for Tony," she said. "He's going to rescue you from the evil king."

"What are you talking about Mae? Who's Tony? What evil king?" I replied.

"Hang tough, Jule. Don't give up, even if you think you can't hold on for one more second. You can do it. You're stronger than you think."

Mae went back to splashing and kicking at the waves. Her rollicking laughter was contagious. Soon we were soaked, dancing with hands clasped in the sun-sparkled water.

Julia wiped a tear as it touched her smiling lips. The soft *knock* at her door startled her. "Yes?"

"Are you all right, Ms. Metcalf?" Ron asked.

"Yes. Thanks, Ron." She neither stood nor opened the door. It was her private moment, and she didn't feel like sharing it, especially with Ron Longstreet. They had no rapport and nothing in common.

It was embarrassing to have someone looking over her shoulder night and day. To know when you laughed or cried at some private thought. And he certainly wasn't her choice of hero and protector. That distinction, along with her heart, belonged to Tony.

At first, Ron had wanted to camp out in her bedroom while she slept — as if she would allow that. After Julia's flat refusal, he satisfied his security duties by checking her room every blessed night before she went to bed. He thoroughly inspected under the bed, inside the closet, out the window, on the roof, and in the bathroom. It drove her to near insanity.

No visitors in, and she wasn't allowed to go out unescorted. The last straw was in the backyard, as he stood fists on hips looking up at her bedroom window. She watched him from the kitchen window as he walked to the garden shed and returned carrying an axe. Panic struck her as she realized his intent.

"No!" she yelled, as she bounded out the back door and rounded the corner of the house. He set the head of the axe on the ground.

"Ms. Metcalf, you need to get back into the house. You're vulnerable out here."

"Just what the hell do you think you're doing?" she demanded. Her face was getting hot, and her jaw was set.

"I'm chopping down these vines and getting rid of this old trellis."

"The hell you are. I made that trellis out of driftwood and willow branches, and the trumpet vine was grafted by my grandfather."

"Well, it winds all the way to your room. Anybody and their dog could climb up there and be in the house in seconds."

She stood in front of it, spreading out to protect it. "No."

Ron ran a hand over his face and sighed. "Look, can't we prune it or something? I mean... it really is a security problem."

"I forbid you to touch it." She looked up the trellis.

His eyebrows shot up, and the sides of his mouth twitched. "You forbid it? Wow."

"I can't believe you were going to just chop it down without even saying anything to me." Her hands were still balled up in fists. She stomped toward him. Her finger jabbed him in the chest. She looked up to meet his gaze. He looked mildly amused. "It's mine, and you have invaded my personal space enough."

He leaned into that personal space, nearly touching nose to nose. "It's my job to keep you safe." His voice was low, resonating with restraint. "You take it down your way, or I'll take it down mine. But one way or the other, it's coming down tomorrow morning."

Something about the look in his eye made her very uncomfortable. She turned and headed for the shed before his eyes could look any further into her heart.

CHAPTER FORTY

LONNY BECK SAT SLUMPED NEXT TO his attorney, staring blankly at the wall. It was painted drab green, and the room had no windows except the small one in the locked steel door. A viewing mirror filled one wall.

Dale had kept him waiting in this stark room for over an hour. Added to that was the processing time to take his fingerprints, mug shot, and fill out paperwork. Beck had to have a powerful hunger by now.

Dale elbowed the door open. In his arms he balanced the file, a plastic container, a bakery bag, and a large drink. He set everything down and opened the food container. The heavenly smell of warm cheesy lasagna filled the small room. From the bag, Dale set out a large double chocolate frosted brownie.

"I didn't have time for lunch. You don't mind, do you?" He smiled and took a big bite of lasagna. The sound of Lonny's stomach growling could almost be heard in the next county.

The lawyer was the first to chime in. "You must be aware

that my client didn't have time for lunch either. I find your behavior distasteful and rude."

"Oh," Dale replied. "I'm sorry. I'll go finish this and come when I'm done." He started to get up, noting that Beck was staring longingly at the lasagna, with the occasional glance at the brownie.

"No," the lawyer said. "We've waited quite long enough." He crossed his arms.

"Okay, your call." Dale settled back in, glancing at Beck. "You want some of this? My wife's lasagna is famous." The fact that he was divorced, and his ex-wife's cooking expertise didn't extend beyond a phone call was irrelevant. He belched quietly for emphasis.

"Disgusting," the lawyer commented.

"Huh. Is that supposed to make me feel bad? Because as I see it, your asinine delays caused the problem. Now, shall we quit wasting time?"

"My client will take the Fifth."

"I haven't asked anything yet," Dale replied waving a forkful of the lasagna, sending another waft of tomatoes and garlic into the air. Beck's stomach gurgled with desire. Dale pushed the plate out of the way and coincidentally, closer to Lonny's face. He opened the file before him.

"Lonny Beck." He looked up at the big man. "You've got an impressive sheet. Looks like you started when you were about sixteen. Petty stuff back then — larceny, misdemeanor theft, assault. But then you graduated to felonies, didn't you? Wasn't that about the time you starting working for Cordell?"

"My client takes the Fifth."

"You do work for Mr. Cordell, don't you Lonny?"

Lonny straightened up and his mouth opened. The attorney nudged him, and he closed it again, resuming his slumped posture.

"My client has nothing to say."

"This is great lasagna. You want a bite, Lonny?" Beck's eyes met the fork longingly and tracked from the container to Dale's mouth ceaselessly. He smacked his lips in anticipation.

"I could probably get you a whole slab if I felt so inclined."

His statement wasn't true, but Dale figured if the guy sang, he'd get him a whole pan of the stuff. As it was, Dale had purchased the piece he was eating from a young patrolman who'd brought it for lunch.

The attorney's eyes rolled. "Just stay quiet, Lonny." He drew Beck's attention to him and looked him square in the eye. "Mr. Cordell wouldn't like it if you said anything. You think about that. You know how Mr. Cordell hates to be unhappy, don't you?"

Beck seemed to shrink in his chair.

Dale took a bite of the brownie. It was sinfully delicious, and his eyes closed in ecstasy. "This brownie is a work of art."

The lawyer huffed and stood. "If we're finished then?"

Dale leaned back and crossed his legs at the ankle. "Sit down. I'll let you know when we're finished."

The lawyer sat abruptly and glared at Dale.

Dale stared at the attorney a moment and then turned his attention back to Lonny. "Where were you on the night of June 15th between the hours of 9:00 p.m. and 3:00 a.m.?"

"How many times must I tell you, Detective? My client will not answer any questions under the protection of the Fifth Amendment."

Dale's attention remained riveted on Beck. "Where was Mr. Cordell on that night, Lonny? I can help you, you know. You could get immunity. I know it wasn't your fault, you were only doing what Mr. Cordell said."

Lonny looked at the lawyer, and then back to Dale. "I was... he was..."

"Enough," the lawyer exclaimed sharply. "For the last

time, my client won't answer any questions."

Dale still didn't break his gaze on Lonny. "We have your DNA and sworn affidavits." He stood abruptly and leaned into Beck's personal space. "You're going down, Beck, and so's your boss."

He stood and gathered up his things. "Deal stands. You turn on Cordell, you go free. Think about it." The door slammed behind him.

Immediately after bail was set, Beck was out and headed back to Nevermore.

CHAPTER FORTY-ONE

"YOU SAID I COULD TAKE IT down my way. This is my way." Julia's arms were crossed. Stubbornness had her raise her chin in Ron's direction.

"Look, I didn't know you were going to climb up on a ladder and make yourself the easiest target on earth."

She looked up at the vine. "What did you think I was going to do, Mr. Longstreet? Zap it down with my laser vision?"

"There's no need to be snide, Ms. Metcalf." His fists were on his hips and his tone exasperated.

"If Cordell tried to kidnap me, then that means he wants me alive, right?"

"Maybe, but I'm certainly not convinced you'd stay that way."

She paused, considering that. "True, but he's not going to shoot me off the ladder, when it'll only take a few minutes to prune."

"You've got five minutes."

"What?"

"Four minutes, forty-five seconds."

"I really don't like you, Mr. Longstreet."

"Love you too, sweetheart."

She flipped him off as she climbed up the ladder. Ten minutes later, Julia wiped the sweat from her brow and the tears from her eyes as she finished pruning back the lovely trumpet vines. Ron had offered to help, but it was something that required her care and attention. She wasn't going to let that goon manhandle her beautiful vine and trellis.

Carefully, she disassembled the upper portion of the trellis and handed him the pieces, which he stacked in the wheelbarrow.

"You about done?" he asked.

"Yes." There was no point in arguing further. The deed was done.

"Just doing my job."

"Yeah."

"Look, I'm sorry you had to cut down your... whatever that thing was. But it looked like it needed cutting back, anyway."

She merely glared and grabbed the wheelbarrow and headed for the shed. He ran to beat her there and checked inside.

"You think someone is hiding in my shed?"

"Well, now that I've looked at it, no." He shook his head disdainfully at the cluttered mess.

Good God. Why does he have to be such a pain in the ass?

CHAPTER FORTY-TWO

DALE WENT BACK TO HIS CUBE for a while to update his murder book and file his report. Only one thing was on his mind — the inch-and-a-half-thick T-bone steak waiting for him in a savory marinade at home. In his mind, he grilled it to mouth-watering perfection. He left the station in a hurry. Maybe some portabella caps to go with the steak. He jingled the keys between his fingers.

Out of the blue, the hairs on the back of his neck stood on end. Just as he turned, pain in his chest spread like fire. The air left his lungs with a *whump*.

He heard a sound that struck fear in his heart. *Oh shit, I've been shot.*

His backside hit the ground with such force that he could feel the rough asphalt as it dug into his flesh.

Something warm spread over his torso. He touched it and looked at his bloodied hand. The toothpick fell from his lips as his head hit the asphalt.

Feet pounded.

People were yelling.

He wished they'd shut up.

"I WANT TO TELL you about my session with Dr. Ingvaldson. Do you have time?"

"Of course." He smiled. "Anything for you."

"I can't shake the feeling something in the dream is important, but I don't know what part."

"Start at the beginning."

"Fair warning — I will likely get emotional. It was very intense."

He took her hand. "Go ahead. Any time you need to stop, we stop."

"Okay. She put me into a hypnotic state. I remember going under, and then suddenly, it was as though I was seeing it through Mae's eyes." She swallowed hard and her eyes became misty.

"Do you want to do this later?"

"No." She took a deep breath and blew it out slowly. "It started out dark. I think it was when Mae was sleeping. She woke up suddenly because there was a large hand over her mouth."

Tony's phone beeped. "One second, Jule."

"Sure." Her hands couldn't keep still.

"Lange," Tony said into his phone while gazing into Julia's eyes. He paled and his mouth dropped open.

"How bad?" His jaw muscles tightened as he listened. He jammed his phone into his pocket.

"It's Dale," he said to Julia.

"What happened?"

"He's been shot. They took him to St. Bart's." The sadness

and worry in his eyes tugged at her heart.

"I'll go with you."

"No, we can't take that chance. Besides, your shadow would never allow it."

"Then I'll sneak away and follow in half an hour. I know where the surgery waiting room is."

"It's safer if you don't. I'll call you." He pecked her cheek and checked the church parking lot. He controlled his gait going out to the car, but she could see that he was stricken with fear.

Father Paul appeared quietly at her side and put an arm around her shoulders. "I'll pray for him, Jule."

Ron waited in the hallway. He had checked out Father Paul's background and the entire church before allowing Julia the hour away from home. He had explained to her that protecting her away from home was more difficult and she shouldn't expect to be able to do it often. She'd resisted punching him in the face.

CHAPTER FORTY-THREE

THE SHOOTER HAD TAKEN CAREFUL AIM. He was the farthest distance he could be from the target for accuracy, which was a couple hundred yards away, perched on the roof of the courthouse. He could've made the shot from much farther away, of course. But with buildings and pedestrians in the path, he had to shoot from the closer vantage point. It also afforded him a reasonable escape route.

He lay on his stomach. The cupola above shaded his hiding spot, making him virtually invisible. He'd been up there the better part of the afternoon, assembling his weapon and checking it over. Now, it was locked and loaded and sighted in on the target's vehicle. The target's shift had ended half an hour before, but he was still nowhere to be seen. The shooter arched his aching back and settled back into position. He checked the scope again.

He could just make out the target as he approached the exit. There was a smile on his face. *I'll wipe off that ill-advised grin*, the shooter thought.

He tracked the target through the scope until he was in the optimal position, right next to his car. The target paused to unlock the door. The crosshairs were right over the target's heart. A thrill ran through the shooter as he squeezed the trigger. The muzzle spat just as the target flinched as though someone pinched him. The shot was off just a fraction.

He swore as he slapped the bolt and cycled another round into the chamber. He immediately took aim again. There was no time for a second shot. But as he checked the scope, he saw a bloody splotch growing quickly over the target's chest as the detective dropped onto his back. Satisfied, he nodded and crawled back away from the edge of the building and looked around for the shell casing. He didn't see it. *Never leave your brass,* rang through his head as it turned from side to side.

No time! He thought. He removed the barrel of the rifle and pitched the halves into his duffel and headed across the roof to the back of the building and the access door.

Once in the stairwell, the shooter stripped off his jumpsuit. He removed a jacket, glasses, and briefcase from the duffel. The disassembled weapon and the folded duffel fit neatly into the briefcase, with the exception of the barrel. He removed the suppressor and screwed on the head of a cane.

The stairwell was clear. Sprinting down the stairs, he checked his watch. *Right on schedule,* he noted. A slight smile played across his face. *I've still got it.* He left the building at a normal pace.

"What's going on?" he asked a passerby.

"A cop was shot, right in the parking lot," the woman explained.

"Oh, wow. Did they get the guy who shot him?"

"No, I don't think so."

"Okay, well. I don't think I'll hang around then."

She stared at him for a beat. He watched as realization hit

her.

"Holy cow!" She paled, and turned to run in the opposite direction.

He laughed softly as got into his car and drove off.

CHAPTER FORTY-FOUR

JULIA SNUCK OUT THE FRONT DOOR of the church to the waiting cab. Her heart pounded with the thrill of having outsmarted both Father Paul and Ron. How could Paul have agreed with Longstreet? She felt betrayed so she had excused herself and gone to the ladies' room, where she called the cab.

Julia asked to be dropped off at the employee parking lot and took the shuttle to the hospital. She snuck in through the kitchen entrance, which smelled of bland food and dish soap then hurried through until an orderly stopped her.

"What are you doing here, lady?"

"I took a wrong turn." She smiled at him and tried to look distracted. "Where's the surgical floor?"

He shook his head and took her arm. Upon swinging open the door, he pointed down the hallway. "Go all the way to the end, and then go left." He pointed in the proper direction. "Go to the information desk and ask for your party. They'll direct you from there."

"Thank you," she said, but he had already retreated into

the kitchen shaking his head.

She hurried to the end of the hallway and made the turn, bypassing the information desk. From past visits to St. Bart's, she knew that the third floor was the surgical floor. The waiting room would be on the right.

Tony stood at the window looking out.

Julia touched his arm. He brushed at his face and turned toward her.

"They just took him into surgery. It doesn't look good." He pursed his lips and looked away.

Her hand slid over his arm. "I'm sorry, Tony. I'm holding a good thought for him."

His long arms wrapped around her and his cheek rested on the top of her head. "Where's Longstreet?"

"Um, he didn't come with me."

He pushed her away so he could look her in the eye. "What? You snuck off?"

"Well, I was careful. I took a cab, and then snuck in through the hospital kitchen."

"Damn. You need to call him. Right now."

"What? I thought you were on my side."

"I am, and so is Longstreet. Now call."

She pressed her lips together and gave Tony a sideways glance, dialed Ron's cell, and told him where she was.

"He's on his way. I'll have to leave when he gets here."

He pulled her close again. "I know. But both he and I need to know you're safe."

"Lange?" A young uniformed officer approached them.

"Yeah, that's me."

"I was told to give you this." He handed Tony a large envelope. It was Dale's preliminary forensic report. The bullet was a .280 rifle round, shot from some distance. *Had to be a decent marksman*, Tony thought. It was likely that it had come from the courthouse across from the precinct.

"Have they processed the suspected source?"

"Ongoing, Detective. They found a shell casing wedged under the decorative edging at the base of the cupola on top of the courthouse."

"That explains why he didn't pick up his brass. No time to look for it, I imagine. Keep me informed and take this to the house." He handed him back the report for delivery to the precinct.

"Dale was my first partner," he said to Julia, his voice shaking. "I was a shithead rookie who knew it all." He smiled briefly, but the sadness in his eyes was telling.

"I'm sorry," she said. "I'm praying for him, Tony."

He hugged her. She rested her cheek up under his chin and held tight.

Longstreet walked briskly toward them. His jaw was set, and his eyes icy.

Tony shook his hand and introduced himself. Ron nodded curtly and stared holes into Julia.

Tony turned to her. "Jule, you've got to go before someone sees you here. Your being here has meant more to me than you can ever know."

"I'll see you later, Tony." She kissed his cheek and walked with Ron to the elevator.

THE SURGERY SEEMED TO last forever. Finally, a nurse came into the waiting room. "Detective Lange?"

"Yeah, that's me."

"He's out of recovery. You can go in for a few minutes if you want, but he likely won't know you're there."

Dale's face was as white as the sheets. He was the nucleus in a web of tubing of various size and function. Machines hummed. The respirator gave off a rhythmic *thump*.

Tony sagged. He wished Julia could be there with him.

Suddenly, an alarm went off and a nurse hustled into the room. "You'll have to leave," she said. She was busy fiddling with the tubes and machines.

"Is he..." Tony began.

"Out."

"But."

"I mean now!"

Several more medical people burst into the room. One of them pushed Tony out into the hallway.

"Clear!" someone yelled. Dale's body contorted in an upward arch.

When the door shut, Tony backed away, staring at it.

A few minutes later, the door to Dale's room opened and an assembly of medical personnel disbursed.

"He's holding his own, for now," the doctor told them. "The next twenty-four hours will be critical."

"Can I stay?" Tony asked.

"Up to you. I'm making no promises, Detective. But he's in good health otherwise. We can always hope."

"He's stubborn. I've heard that helps."

"That's right. He'll need all the stubborn he's got."

The doctor's words seemed to echo in the empty hallway. Tony stood there helplessly, feeling utterly alone.

CHAPTER FORTY-FIVE

BY THE END OF THE WEEK, Ron had reorganized Julia's entire house. He was certain she wanted to choke the life out of him. Still, he hoped she had become accustomed to, and part of him wished she would become dependent on, his presence.

She obviously missed Tony, but she wouldn't risk seeing him again. Ron made it abundantly clear to her that they still had not caught her assailant. It looked like the older detective's shooting was related. Since they could no longer meet in person, Tony called frequently on the disposable cell phone and Julia spent a good deal of time in her studio.

Strands of Julia's hair fell in wisps around her face as she worked. She was completely focused, unaware of Ron's presence. Her frown told him she was displeased with her creation.

When her hand slapped her welding helmet back over her face, he averted his eyes. Under other circumstances, he might have pursued his attraction to her, but he was her protection. Giving in to some silly unrequited crush would only break his concentration and leave her vulnerable.

He heard the torch shut off and peeked around the doorway. A smile graced her face. It made his heart clench, followed closely by his jaw. He turned back to the house angry with himself. Why couldn't he get her out of his mind? It was just a job *and* she had somebody.

He shook his head. It must have been the heat from the welder that set her face aglow. He sighed impatiently and cleaned his weapon again.

"Ron?"

He jumped and dropped a couple of bullets on the floor. "What?"

"Sorry, I didn't mean to startle you."

"What did you want?" Damn it. If she could sneak up on him, so could her enemies. He pretended to focus on the pieces of his pistol.

"I need some muscle in the studio. Do you have a minute?"

He glanced up at her. "Fine."

He helped position a heavy wheel onto the enclosed bench she used for a paint booth.

"Thanks," she said softly. She smiled at him. It was the first time she looked genuinely pleased with him.

"Try to keep in mind that I'm here to keep you safe, not fetch and carry."

He left her with her mouth hanging open.

"What did I do?" he heard her say as he crossed the back yard.

LATER THAT EVENING, RON poked his head into the kitchen. "Ms. Metcalf?"

"Can't you just call me Julia?"

"No. I thought I should let you know that I have asked for reassignment. My replacement will be here tomorrow, noon." Part of him wanted to leave that very moment, and part wanted her to beg him to stay. Her eyes went wide, but she said nothing. He turned to go back to the den.

"Ron?"

"Yeah?"

"What have I done to make you angry enough to leave? I mean, I know I can be a pain, and after the trellis thing, I guess I can't blame you. I'd just like to know…"

"It doesn't matter." He turned and walked away.

It does to me, she thought.

CHAPTER FORTY-SIX

DALE'S EYELIDS FELT LIKE LEAD. HE couldn't open them though he tried until he was exhausted.

Awareness came and went. At times, he could hear people talking, but couldn't quite get what they were saying. He tried to talk to them, but nothing happened. He tried waving his arms. Again nothing. Was that Tony's voice he heard?

"Damn it boy, get the mush out of your mouth so I can understand you," he said. But he felt no vibration in his throat and no sound came to his ears.

Twice, he saw a white light. He was drawn to it on some level, but felt confused. He knew the light meant peace and contentment, which sounded kind of dull, so he turned away.

Someone was squeezing his hand, and he was finally able to understand what Tony was saying. He mustered all of his will and squeezed back.

"YOUR PARTNER IS IN a coma, Detective Lange," the nurse said tersely. "He can't answer your questions."

"They say people who are comatose understand, or at least are aware people are there. I figure if I bounce some of these ideas off him, it might spark some interest. Besides," he said with a charming smile, "I need him to close this case quick. The rest of my life depends on it."

The nurse merely rolled her eyes and checked the IV. Tony patiently waited until she left, and took Dale's hand.

"Come on, Buddy. You gotta fight, and fight hard. We nearly lost you twice, and that's not happening again. You fight with everything you've got, you hear me? I need you to be my best man."

Tony wasn't sure at first that the pressure he felt was more than nerve movement, but the second time, it was weak but steady. His eyes grew wide.

"Come on back, Dale. You can do it."

He released Dale's hand and grabbed for the door. "Nurse!" he yelled toward the nurse's station. "Nurse!"

Immediately, she jumped to her feet and bustled toward him. "You hush, Detective. There are sick people on this floor who need their rest, and your yelling is very upsetting to them. One more outburst like that and you're off my floor. Got it?"

He nodded silently.

"Now what's the problem?"

"He moved. He squeezed my hand." It was all Tony could do not to yell it out, along with a robust 'hallelujah'.

She smirked. "Comatose patients often get nerve pulses. It may not be an indicator that the patient is coming out of their coma, but I'll check on him for you. Wait out here. Quietly."

She stabbed a finger at Tony and went in to examine Dale.

A few minutes later, Tony heard her speaking. "Welcome back, Mr. Melhus. You had us worried for a while."

Tony's eyes and grin widened as he strode through the door. "You old fart, you scared me half to death," he exclaimed. Dale's eyes lit up as he saw Tony, but his attention was immediately drawn back to the nurse.

Her eyes narrowed as her gaze darted to Tony. "I told you to wait outside. I'd suggest you do it, now." Her hands were on her hips, and her face was pinched and harsh. He backed out slowly, defeated by a formidable opponent.

Tony paced nervously while two more nurses and a doctor entered Dale's room and shut the door behind them. The only glimpse into the room was of the exam curtain. One of the nurses came out of the room carrying a covered tray. Finally, the doctor came out. Tony had to stop him to get a status update.

"Well?" Tony demanded.

"Your friend is a very stubborn man."

"Yeah, I told you before that he was. You don't know the half of it, Doc."

"We've removed the ventilator as he made it quite clear that it was coming out one way or another. We'll watch him for the next twelve hours. If we don't have to put it back in by then, he'll probably be okay. I'll sedate him if I think it's best. Don't get him all riled up. He could still easily backslide." With that the doctor turned and walked away.

Tony peeked into the room just as the nurse pulled the curtain aside. She eyed him suspiciously. "Five minutes, Detective. Not one more."

He nodded and approached Dale's bed cautiously. His eyes were closed. "Melhus? Are you in there?"

Dale's eyed fluttered open. "What the fuck happened? I can't remember a damn thing." His voice rasped like it hurt something fierce.

"Sniper. Off the courthouse roof."

"No shit. How bad?"

"They had to jump start you twice."

"Fuckin' A." Dale's eyes rolled.

"Hey, Buddy, you get some rest. I'm gonna make tracks before Nurse Ratchet comes back," Tony said.

One side of Dale's mouth twitched.

"I heard that, Detective," the nurse said through tight jaws.

"Lange," Dale whispered.

"Yeah?"

"Sneak me in a pack of Marlboros."

"And suffer the wrath of Ratchet? No can do, my friend." Tony turned and caught the ghost of a smile on the nurse's face.

"See you tomorrow."

CHAPTER FORTY-SEVEN

IN THE DEAD OF NIGHT, THE two figures silently scaled the back fence and crouched in the bushes surveying Julia's back yard. The slender one signaled to the larger of the two. With astounding grace, the big man traversed the yard without a sound. The smaller man followed and paused at the back door. He removed an electronic device from his pocket and held it near the security pad. After a few seconds, the lock popped open and the pair snuck into the kitchen.

"Milbert?" the big man whispered.

Milbert made a slashing motion across his throat with his hand. They had watched and listened for several days before the break in. They knew that Ron was staying in the den, which was only steps from where they stood now. He held up a finger and closed the space between the kitchen and the den in a blink.

WHAT WAS THAT? RON silently bolted from the daybed while shoving a pillow under the blankets where his body had lain a split second before. The boards on the rear porch creaked again, ever so slightly. Longstreet took his position with his weapon drawn. Just in case, he tucked his clutch piece in the rear waistband of his sweats. He heard the back door *click*, but the alarm never sounded. *Jammer,* he thought. Must be pretty high tech. He heard whispering, but couldn't make out the words. Ron tensed, coiled like a spring.

The door opened slightly and the barrel of a Walther PPK with a silencer fitted to its tip appeared. Two shots spat fire into the darkness. Feathers flew. The door slowly swung open, and the profile of a slight but fit man came into view.

Ron's fist met with his jaw with such force that the man's neck cracked in protest. Hennings' leg was up and swinging at him in the same motion. His rubber-soled shoe clipped Ron's nose, breaking it like glass, and sending Longstreet's weapon skittering across the room.

Jesus, he's fast, Ron thought. The sound of bone breaking and the feel of blood flowing from his smashed nose distracted him for a moment. He shook his head to clear it.

A rabbit punch blackened his right eye. Ron's vision swam as he struggled to gain control. Another blow to the ribs shot pain through Ron's torso. *Who is this guy?* he thought.

"Is this the person they sent to protect Ms. Metcalf? An incompetent?" Hennings smiled.

Ron's breath came in ragged gasps. He leaned against the wall with his hands pressed to his thighs.

Hennings' evil laugh made Ron want to shove it right down his throat. He bided his time.

"The only question is, do I play with you for a while, or just kill you now?"

Ron raised a hand. "Look mister, I don't know what you want, but you win." He straightened a bit, and pretended to examine his ribs. Slowly his other hand crept around to the small of his back.

"You're a coward. There will be no pleasure in killing you. It won't stop me from doing it, but I'd prefer to kill a formidable opponent."

Just another half inch. Ron felt the cold metal brush his fingertips. Suddenly, he lunged forward and knocked Hennings off balance. In a flash, the pistol was in Ron's hand and swinging around to Hennings' head.

Just as he fired, Hennings dropped to the ground and swept Ron's feet out from under him. He grabbed Ron's free wrist and chopped at it. It snapped and broke under Hennings' martial arts expertise. The clutch piece slid under the daybed.

Ron stood and curled his good fist around the front of Hennings' shirt and hauled him up off the floor. He roared as he threw Hennings across the room and into the window, shattering the glass.

Ron dropped to the floor and grabbed his pistol. Hennings snarled and ran headlong toward Ron, catching him in the gut. The shards of glass that covered Milbert caught in the dim light like evil snowflakes as they flew into Ron's face and eyes. He stepped back clutching at them.

I've got to get to Julia, he thought desperately.

Hennings pointed the Walther he had retrieved somewhere during the fight. "Goodbye, Mister Security. You have failed."

"Goodbye," Ron replied as he swung his weapon around. Simultaneous shots rang out.

CHAPTER FORTY-EIGHT

JULIA FELT TENSE AND IRRITABLE. SHE couldn't sleep. She tried everything: counting sheep, deep breathing, meditation, reading, but nothing helped. Her mind wouldn't stop. As a last desperate resort, she took a sleeping pill and finally fell into a deep dreamless haze.

She became vaguely aware that something was dreadfully wrong. As she fought to clear her head, the hair on the back of her neck stood up, and at first, she thought she had dreamt something horrible again. Her session with Dr. Ingvaldson still weighed heavily on her heart and mind.

Her insides clenched when she heard glass shatter. She swiftly rolled off the edge of the bed to hide on the floor. Too late she realized that her phone still sat on the table on the other side of the bed.

Why isn't the alarm ringing?

Footsteps were coming closer. In her mind, she gauged their position then jumped up from her hiding spot to lock the door. Her fingers just touched it as the door sprang open sending her sprawling into the bedside table. Pain shot up her arm as she landed in a heap on the floor with her back to the enormous man.

"Don't fight me lady," the intruder demanded. "I'd just as soon not kill you. Mr. Cordell wants you alive."

She lay still, wondering where Ron was. As she started to push up from the floor, she caught a glimpse of her phone lying under the bed. She let her body drop back to the floor.

"Give me a moment, please," she said. "I've hurt my arm. I won't run. I promise."

She heard the sound of a pistol being cocked. "No, you won't."

Her fingers closed around the phone and she deftly drew her arm under her, stuffing the phone down her pants as she slowly got up. She turned slowly and looked the man over.

He was enormous. Even in the dimly lit confines of her room, she could just make out the faint striations on his face. Her heart jumped as realization came to her. This was the man she saw in the dream that Dr. Ingvaldson helped her remember. This was the animal that killed Mae. Fear gripped her.

Suddenly, her phone began to ring. Her face reddened as Lonny stared at her crotch.

He pointed the gun at her head. "Take it out and throw it across the room."

She glanced at the screen. "It's the alarm company," she said. "If I don't answer it, they'll dispatch the police." Her thumb moved slightly to hover over the talk button, hoping he would let her answer.

A shot rang out. Or was it two? Her eyes closed and she waited for death to find her. When it didn't, she assumed it was Longstreet. She just wasn't sure whether or not he was on the receiving end.

Lonny looked at the phone and laughed. "Throw it, now.

We'll be long gone when the police arrive." She obediently threw the phone onto the bed. He grabbed her roughly and bound her hands with a plastic zip tie.

"Please Lonny, it's cold outside." She shivered at the thought of going outside in bare feet and thin pajamas.

"Shut up and keep moving. Hey, how do you know my name?"

"I know about Mr. Cordell, too."

He pointed the gun at her but said nothing.

"My slippers are just there. Can't I put them on?" she asked.

"Hurry up."

She shuffled toward them and slid her feet inside.

"My jacket's in the closet." She started in that direction.

"No. The van is warm enough."

"Are you taking me to the wine cellar at Mr. Cordell's, where you took Mae?"

He stared at her in disbelief. "How do you know that?"

"I know. There are lots of things I know. You better leave now."

He pushed her. The last thing she remembered was something hitting her head for just a split second.

CHAPTER FORTY-NINE

HENNINGS GRABBED HIS SHOULDER, ANGRY THAT he had flinched. The bullet had gone all the way through. That was good; no doctors would be necessary. Ron was slumped on the floor, barely alive.

"Julia," he murmured.

"She's mine now." Hennings raised his weapon and shot Ron through the heart. He'd made it personal.

As he left the den, Hennings glanced up the stairs. Lonny had Julia's limp form slung over his shoulder.

"You haven't damaged her, have you?"

"No Milbert, she fainted."

"Put her down."

Hennings gave her a cursory exam, feeling the lump on her head, and scowled at Lonny. "How many times must I tell you?"

"Honest, Milbert. She fell."

"Put her in the van, and you'd best pray she'll be alright. Mr. Cordell needs her alive."

Julia was thrown onto the back seat of the windowless van with her arms and legs bound. She had regained consciousness, but her head pounded and she felt dizzy. Still, she couldn't give up.

"Lonny, aren't you going to buckle my seat belt? Mr. Cordell would be angry if anything happened, wouldn't he?"

Beck huffed and leaned over her to buckle the restraint. As he did, she bit him hard on the face. An angry guttural noise escaped him as he rammed his elbow into her ribs.

"What the hell is going on back there?" Hennings asked from behind the wheel.

"The bitch bit me," Beck complained as he backhanded her across the mouth, bloodying her lip. He grabbed a roll of duct tape from under the seat and tore off a strip. The brute slapped it over her mouth, catching a chunk of hair so that she could only see to her left.

"Stop damaging her, Lonny. Mr. Cordell will be upset."

Beck narrowed his eyes at her. He slammed the door and got into the front seat as Hennings turned to speak to her before driving off. "I would suggest you stop irritating Mr. Beck. I won't stop him from killing you again. Do we understand each other?"

Julia nodded. She quietly began to work at her restraints. There was no give in either of the zip ties used to bind her hands and feet so she began to work the duct tape with her tongue.

The van stopped briefly as the front gate of Nevermore slowly swung open then continued down the sweeping drive to the mansion. It was an ominous-looking place in the daylight, let alone in the middle of the night. She fought tears.

They'll never get to me fast enough, she thought.

CHAPTER FIFTY

"YOU KNOW, JULIA WAS THE ONLY girl I ever really kissed." Paul smiled at the memory. He and Tony chatted while waiting for Julia and Ron to arrive.

"Really? I thought you priests gave up lust and all that shit."

Paul laughed. "It was before I became a priest."

"Well there must be more to the story."

Paul leaned back and thought a moment. "Julia and Mae were seniors. Mae had men and boys alike courting her from an early age. But Julia was different. She went to public school, unlike Mae. She was shy and quirky even then. But she often lamented that she would likely never get to a school dance.

"No one had asked her the week before, and I overheard her talking to Mae. She had mustered the courage to ask one of the football players that she apparently had quite a crush on."

"I take it the fool turned her down."

"The asshole laughed in her face."

"Oh shit."

"So, I offered to take her."

"And the two of you went?"

"Yes, we did. I was in my second year at the Seminary, but no one there knew anything other than I was her handsome college escort."

"Very nice. And the kiss?"

"Well, all good things come to an end. I took her home, and when I walked her to the door, it just seemed the thing to do. It lasted far longer than I intended. I couldn't help myself."

"I understand that completely."

"She looked at me with a strange little smile. Then you know what she said?"

"What?"

"'Thank you for the best evening of my life, Paul. I'll never, ever forget it. Please don't take this the wrong way, but go back to the Seminary. I don't want to go to Hell.'"

Both men laughed. "What I never told her was that kiss made me seriously consider leaving the Seminary."

"I can believe that. The woman can kiss."

"Wow, look at the time. Give her a call."

Tony tried her number.

"No answer?"

"Nope."

"I'm worried," Paul said. "She's been late a time or two, but never more than a few minutes. Maybe I should go over to her house and check."

"No, we'll go."

They covered the few blocks between the church and Julia's house in a matter of seconds. From the street, everything looked fine. They circled around to the alley behind Julia's house. Tony got out of the car and peeked through the gate. The backdoor stood open. He yanked out his cell and called 911. Once Johnson was on the way, he drew out his weapon.

The sun glinted on something in the side yard. Paul appeared behind him, startling him. Tony pointed to the alley, indicating that Paul was to wait out there. Paul shook his head. Tony narrowed his eyes as he silently snuck through the back gate. As he neared the slivers of broken glass, panic caught his heart.

He pointed to the ground indicating the Father Paul should stay there. Paul firmly shook his head again. Tony pointed to the floor of the porch. His eyes made it clear there would be no further compromise.

Father Paul nodded his agreement to stay there.

Tony pushed the door open with his elbow, pistol at the ready, and tiptoed through the kitchen. He stopped and listened. The smell of blood invaded his nostrils. Fear gripped him. The kitchen, dining room, and living room were clear. He paused at the door to the den and listened. Nothing. But the smell of blood was stronger here.

He carefully opened the door and peered inside. Ron's foot was extended into his line of vision. Poking his head around the corner, he saw instantly that Ron was dead.

He drew in a deep breath and let it out slowly as he continued his search for Julia. The stairs creaked slightly as he slowly ascended them. Climbing the sides of the treads silenced the noise. He paused at the top of the stairs with his pistol at the ready. No sound, no indication of anyone came to him. Julia's bedroom door was slightly ajar. He elbowed it open pointing the pistol right and left. The room was devoid of human life. No Julia, no one. He quickly cleared the rest of the house.

Tony heard the arrival of the backup he'd called for and yelled down to them. "Johnson?"

"Lange? What the hell are you doing here?"

"I came over to make sure Ms. Metcalf was all right. I couldn't reach her by phone, and her priest was concerned."

He bounded down the steps.

"Who's the guy we're holding at gunpoint in the back yard?"

"Father Paul from St. Ann's. He's with me." Tony holstered his pistol.

"Okay. What have we got?"

"DB in the den downstairs named Ronald Longstreet. He's from the Blair Agency, Ms. Metcalf's bodyguard. Shot, beaten. She's not here, so I can only assume she's been taken."

"Shit."

"Yeah. I'm going to check her journals. She has precognitive dreams. There might be a clue there." He looked up the stairs.

"You believe in that shit?"

Lange's eyes met Johnson's. "I didn't until I met Ms. Metcalf. She's the real deal."

"Huh." Johnson looked around. "Have at it. The rest of us have plenty to do. Let me know if you get anything."

"Will do." He turned to go back up the stairs, but stopped halfway up. "Hey Johnson? Did you find anything on Hennings?"

"Not much so far. He has a service record from the Vietnam era. No specifics yet."

"See if you can get a lock on Julia's phone."

Johnson feigned a hurt expression. "Who's running this case, Lange?"

Tony raised his eyebrows.

"Already in the works," Johnson replied.

Tony returned to the bookcase in Julia's room and withdrew the most recent journal. He skimmed through a few pages as he walked back out to the backyard where he would be out of the way. "Sign this out to me and I'll let you know if I find anything." Johnson nodded.

Tony settled into a lawn chair while they processed the

house for forensic evidence. There were no prints, but they were able to glean a few things from the scene. He knew it would be a fair chunk of time to transport the body and comb for trace evidence.

He ran a hand over the cover of the journal. Guilt crawled into his heart as he opened it. These were her personal thoughts and feelings, her dreams. Part of him felt as though he were intruding, but he needed help to find her. They'd killed Mae and they wouldn't hesitate to kill Julia once they'd gotten what they wanted.

The entry from two days prior read: "*So many flowers. The air was thick with the fragrance. The colors were so vivid. They were all swaying in the breeze. I noticed out of the corner of my eye that they were starting to wilt. Soon, all of the stems bent over in profound sadness. I lay down in the garden and wept. The world has changed irrevocably.*"

Tony's heart was heavy. He turned the page, and a smile played across his lips. He touched the words as he read: "*I never dreamed I'd find my heart's desire. I always thought that romance was for younger women. This is the first time in my life that I've been deathly afraid of losing someone. Tony is perfect for me. He's kind and attentive without being intrusive. To him, I am just fine the way I am. I hope I don't scare him off. So often, independent women do. Mother used to say that men need to be needed. I shall resolve to need Tony for everything I can think of. I'm so in love with him.*"

He wasn't sure if he should laugh, cry, or be frightened out of his wits. He closed the book and took it with him to the precinct.

CHAPTER FIFTY-ONE

"LANGE," CAPTAIN ROARK YELLED.

"Yeah, Boss?"

"Get in here, for crissake."

Tony stood nervously in the doorway of the captain's cramped office. "Dale's out of the coma."

"So I heard. You know his password?"

"Yeah."

"Good. Use it. Get his notes and help with the Arbeson case. Any trace at the Metcalf woman's house?"

Tony merely looked down.

"Goddamn it, Lange. You've been seeing her haven't you?"

"I'm sorry, Cap. I just couldn't stay away. She's some kind of special."

"Blah blah blah. Get the notes and give 'em to Johnson. Why couldn't you stay the fuck away from her?"

"We were very discreet, Cap."

"Jesus H. Christ. Help Johnson, but nothing goes in your

name, you hear me?"

"Yes, sir."

Tony took the notes and began to work the evidence. He began by running background checks on all of the principles in Dale's files.

Tony looked through the background information Dale had gathered on Albert Cordell and Lonny Beck. His notes were thorough. Neither Cordell nor Beck possessed the sharpshooting ability it had taken to make the shot that took Dale out. He ran a hand through his hair and got up to get another cup of coffee.

He blew across his mug to cool the thick dark swill that passed as police coffee then resumed his perusal of Dale's reports. *Who is this Milbert guy?* He thought. His fingers flew over the keys. Hennings, Milbert. Approximate age: fifty-five to sixty. Five feet, eight inches tall, about a hundred sixty pounds. Dale's notes indicated he was lean and physically fit. He carried himself with the posture of someone who may have been military.

Tony dug a little deeper. He glanced over his shoulder. No one was paying the slightest attention. He typed in a user ID he shouldn't have had. He had gotten it from an informant and wasn't sure it would even work. He sat back in surprise as Hennings military record materialized on his screen. Hennings had been a highly decorated Green Beret sharp shooter in the Vietnam conflict. His rank had gone as high as Major until he was busted down to Sergeant near the end of his tour. Tony clicked on the details of his service record. The word *Classified* flashed across his screen. "What the...?"

"I heard you have been assigned to me. Does that mean I have to get you flowers for Admin's Day?" Johnson leaned on the top of the cube.

Tony jumped in surprise and closed his laptop. "You scared the crap out of me."

"I'm a detective, Lange. And I detect you may have something on your laptop that you don't want me to see?"

"Anything from Julia's place?"

"We'll know in a while. Quit changing the subject. What have you got?"

"Not much. I was just going through Dale's notes. Take a look at this."

Tony opened the laptop. Johnson leaned in and looked over the screen. "Yeah, that's what I meant — locked up. Let me make a call." Johnson pulled out his cell and dialed.

"You have military clearance?"

"Nah. My sister works at ATF." Johnson turned his attention to the phone. "Shell? I need some 411." He gave her the information and listened. "Really? Huh. Okay, thanks."

"Well?"

"Confirmed, no access to the file. But she did tell me that JAG was involved in his bust down to Sergeant."

"I think we need to talk to Mr. Hennings."

"Sorry, pal. *I* need to talk to Hennings. You stay here and dig. We need way more to put these people away."

"Let's hope it's before they kill anyone else."

"Ten-four, buddy."

Tony turned his attention back to the computer screen before him. "Who are you, Hennings?" Since he was unable to access Milbert's past, he began to look through Beck's arrest record.

Beck had been arrested seventeen times. He started young, with charges of petty larceny, and a car theft as a juvenile.

The rest of the sheet was repetitious, and Tony couldn't keep his mind off the journal lying on the chair across from him.

He sighed and picked it up. He opened to an entry that was from a few days prior and chronicled her session with Dr.

Ingvaldson. As Tony read it, he realized this was what he had been looking for.

Tony called Johnson. "High tail it back upstairs. I've got something."

He ran through the Homicide Department and exploded through the Captain's door without bothering to wait for Johnson.

"I know where they are," Tony stated.

"Detective, to what do I owe this outburst?" The captain folded his hands on his desk.

"I know where the Arbeson boy and Julia Metcalf are being held."

He sighed. "How do you know?"

Tony sat down, taking an extra second to form his pitch. He laid the journal on the desk in front of him. "I strongly suspect they're being held in the wine cellar at Nevermore."

The captain ran a hand over his face. "Please don't tell me your basis is that journal. I've heard all the weird crap I can stand about Ms. Metcalf. We can't get a warrant based on hooey."

"Well, the journal does describe the wine cellar pretty vividly. But I do have something else."

"Spill it."

"Cordell's butler..." he began.

"Oh, sweet Jesus. Now you're gonna tell me the butler did it? Get the hell out of here, Lange. Where's Johnson? Somebody get this nincompoop out of my office."

"Hear me out, Cap. Milbert Hennings was a federal operative. The kind with a classified file. He's a sharpshooter. He's a martial arts expert. And there's the connection to Cordell."

"Where's the proof? I need something to give to the judge to compel him to sign a search warrant. And how the hell did you get all of this information?"

Tony smiled. "I did some research. And Johnson's sister works at ATF. She ran it. It came back classified."

"What kind of research?"

"Ah… I'd rather not say."

"La la la. I cannot hear you." The captain put his hands over his ears.

"Anyway, the report is back from CSI on the scene from the courthouse. Guess who's partial they lifted from the shell casing they found up on the cupola?"

The captain sat up straighter and smiled. "Well, why didn't you say so?" He picked up the phone.

Tony went down to City Records and pulled the building permits for Nevermore. Included should have been a complete set of blueprints. There were obviously some missing from the file, but he was able to clearly discern the entrance to the wine cellar. It was down the stairs from the huge gourmet kitchen. The kitchen was equipped to cook for upwards of 200, although it had probably never happened. Cordell was a recluse and to anyone's knowledge had never entertained on such a grand scale.

Tony copied the blueprints and hurried back upstairs to Homicide. He hit Johnson over the head with the rolled up copies. "Guess what I have here?"

"February's centerfold?"

"Good guess, but no." He shook the roll at Johnson.

"A treasure map?"

"Of sorts. It's the blueprints for the main residence at Nevermore."

"Smart thinking, Lange."

He tapped his own head with the roll, and was about to unroll them onto Johnson's desk when two men in dark suits hustled through Homicide and into Captain Roark's office. Tony and Johnson looked at each other.

"Feds," they said simultaneously.

"I got FBI, five bucks," Tony said.

"Nah, Homeland Security," Johnson countered as they unrolled the copies.

They were just getting a feel for the place when they heard Roark bellow their names.

"Shit." Again, simultaneously.

They trudged into the captain's cramped office.

"Shut the door," Roark demanded.

"What's going on, Cap?" Johnson asked.

"These gentlemen are from the FBI. They have an interest in your case."

"I'm Special Agent Rogness, and this is Agent Vasquez. We understand you're looking at a man named Milbert Hennings."

Five dollars changed hands before they acknowledged the suits.

"We've just gotten a warrant to search his place of residence," Johnson replied.

"You realize he lives at Nevermore."

"Yes."

"We're having your warrant rescinded."

Tony jumped to his feet. "Whoa, there are hostages in there. You can't endanger those people."

"Look, we've been told you can't prove the hostages are there, and we have a federal warrant, which trumps yours. If we happen across your alleged hostages, we'll do what we can to protect them. But in the grand scheme of things, our case takes precedence."

Tony's gut twisted with rage. "What the hell could be so damned important that two innocent people no longer matter?"

"That's classified."

Tony lunged toward the closest fed and got up in his face. "That's unacceptable. This Milbert shithead shot one of our own." He stabbed a finger into the first fed's chest. "He's aided and abetted his boss in kidnapping two people. He'll kill them once he's gotten what he wants."

Both feds responded with stony silence. Finally, Special Agent Rogness turned to Roark. "I trust you'll keep your boys in check."

"When is your op going down?" Roark asked.

"Classified. Keep your people out of our way for the next forty-eight hours."

"Forty-eight hours? They'll be dead by then." Tony's voice shook with rage. His fists were balled up and he had a hard time keeping them at his side. Johnson stepped between Tony and the feds to keep them out of harm's way.

The two agents turned and left silently. Tony leaned over Roark's desk. "That's it? They walk out of here and we let them? Those people are gonna die, Cap. We're here to protect and serve." Hot tears threatened and Tony turned away.

Roark stared at him a moment. "I got a favor coming to me. Let me see if we can wangle an invitation to the fed's party."

Johnson smiled. "Yes, sir." He turned to leave, and Tony got up to follow.

"Tony, stay here. I want to talk to you," the captain said.

"Sir?"

Once the door closed, Roark leaned back in his chair. "Look, Lange. Your behavior was unprofessional."

"But sir…"

"Shut up. I'm not done."

"Yes, sir." Tony hung his head.

"You pissed those guys off royally."

"How could you tell?"

Roark chuckled. "I know your girl's there, and the Arbeson kid. I'm gonna stick my neck out on this, Lange. Don't get my head chopped off, you got it?"

"Yes, sir." Tony went to find Johnson.

A few moments later, Roark called them back in. "We're in, but only as observers."

Johnson put a finger in his ear and shook it. "Didn't catch all of that. You said we're in?"

Roark smiled. "Let's roll. They're staging as we speak."

The ride to Nevermore seemed to take days. Tony cracked his knuckles and checked his weapon for the umpteenth time. Johnson had gotten them a spot at the servant's entrance, far from the two jerks that had paid them a visit, and more importantly, close to the cellar access. The blueprints told them everything they needed to know about the layout.

They met their contact at the side gate and were told to wait until the entrance team had secured the premises before entering.

CHAPTER FIFTY-TWO

SETH AND JULIA SAT WITH THEIR arms and legs bound to their chairs. Their muscles ached after having been tied there for hours. Her face and scalp still stung from Lonny's ruthless removal of the duct tape. She fought hot tears of fear and anger fruitlessly.

"How could you be so uncaring?" she whispered to Seth. "She loved you, and she tried so hard to be a good mother to you. Your father wouldn't hear it. That was why you had a governess, he'd say. You were given no boundaries whatsoever."

Seth's head hung.

They heard the sound of keys clattering just before the door at the top of the stairs opened.

Milbert descended the stairs carrying some papers. "Ms. Metcalf."

Julia jutted out her chin defiantly, but said nothing.

"I have some papers for you to sign. You will sign over the Arbeson Trust to Seth immediately. There will be no

215

discussion, no second chance. You will sign or you will die. It's just that simple. Do you understand?"

"Why don't you just kill me? Seth would gain control of the Trust eventually." She studied him a moment. "But then you'd have to wait for probate, wouldn't you?" A smile crept over her face. "That could take years with an estate this big. Assuming I haven't already had my own will rewritten."

He smiled briefly. "None of that matters. The papers I have for you to sign are legal and binding. One is to relinquish the Arbeson Trust, and the other is your last will and testament. You will sign one or the other. Your choice."

"And if I sign neither?"

"That would be my pleasure." An evil smile spread across his face. "I'll give you some time to decide." He climbed the stairs, still smiling.

Once the upstairs door closed, Julia lowered her voice again and turned to Seth. "How could you?"

"I swear, Julia," Seth said. "I didn't know they would kill her."

His eyes darted fearfully around the dank and dim cellar. Racks of wine bottles, covered in dust, filled most of the room. They sat in the center in an unfurnished area.

"They were just gonna kidnap her and hold her for ransom," he continued.

"Are you that naïve? Couldn't you guess the thugs to whom you owed all that money were connected to very dangerous people?" The tears flowed freely now.

"Honest, Julia. It seemed like the answer to my problems, but they just kept wanting more and more." He hung his head.

"Yeah, that's how it usually works." Her voice softened.

"Shut up down there." A deep voice bellowed from the top of the stairs.

Lonny came down the stairs. "You two better shut up before Mr. Cordell hears you. You don't want to make him mad."

"Lonny? You murdered Mae, didn't you? It started here in the wine cellar, but you dragged her off to the woods, didn't you?" Julia accused.

Lonny stopped in his tracks and stared at her. "How do you know this stuff?"

"I know, Lonny." Her mind conjured a plan that she hoped would work. "Just like I know Mr. Cordell plans to get rid of you."

His head whipped around. His hand struck her face like a sledgehammer. "He'd never do that. Never."

Slowly, she turned back around. Her entire head felt like it would explode. "He doesn't appreciate all the things you do for him, does he, Lonny?" Her speech slurred with the swelling and a rivulet of blood dribbled from the corner of her mouth.

Lonny just stared.

"He's always finding fault, isn't he?" she persisted.

He jerked her arm. "Shut up. Just shut up." His fists clenched.

"Shut up, Julia," Seth urged. "You're pissing him off."

"Lonny, you know I have a lot of money, right? I could make you a very rich man. You wouldn't have to take that kind of abuse from Mr. Cordell. Think about it." Her head was swimming. Nausea filled her and threatened to launch the contents of her stomach without prejudice.

"No!" he cried as his hand came around and struck the other side of her face so hard that the bruises started to color almost immediately. She was near fainting when a man's voice made a shiver run up her spine.

"What's going on down here?" Down the stairs glided Albert Cordell, in a tailored Italian suit, impeccably groomed.

Cordell glanced sharply at the thug and pointed to a small table hidden in the shadows. Lonny sprang into action and began dragging the table noisily across the stone floor toward where the tidy man stood. He covered his ears with his manicured hands. "Lon, please."

"Oh, sorry," he replied as he picked the table up and lugged it closer.

He set it down and blew the dust from its surface, sending a swirling cloud into the air. Cordell pulled a sharply creased handkerchief from his pocket and placed it over his mouth and nose while waving at Lon. Immediately, the thug pulled a dirty bandana from his pocket and flapped it around trying to clear the air. He then wiped the table with it, and backed away submissively.

The man gave him a harsh look and turned his attention back to his prisoners. His slender fingers set a briefcase on the table and worked the clasps. From the case he retrieved a pair of fitted black leather gloves. Carefully, he worked each hand into one of them, taking his time. When he finished, he flexed his hands while never breaking eye contact with Julia.

She stiffened, and her eyes grew wide as she swayed in the chair.

"She's the one who inherited," Seth said hastily. "I have no control over any of it. Not even—"

The backhanded slap stopped him cold. Julia's heart slammed into her throat. Tears threatened, but she shoved them back.

"Shut up, you impudent cretin." He looked Julia over. "Lon, did you damage Ms. Metcalf?"

"She made me mad."

Cordell sighed. "You were told not to damage her, weren't you?"

"Yes, but she told me lies about you." Lon began to back away from Cordell. "She said you were gonna get rid of me. She said you were a bad man. She told me she'd give me money if I helped her escape." He shuffled his feet. "She's a witch. She knows stuff."

"What sort of stuff?"

"Like where I took Mrs. Arbeson. And she knew about this place."

"Thank you Lon. That will be all." He turned his intense gaze back to Julia. Blood dripped from her mouth, and her face was already black and blue.

"I must apologize for Mr. Beck's actions. He sometimes doesn't know his own strength. Now, shall we talk?"

He moved very close to Julia, staring straight into her soul. It was clear to her that his was as black as night.

"I'm quite charmed to finally have the opportunity to get to know you, Ms. Metcalf."

He reached over and grabbed Seth's ear and twisted viciously. Seth cried out and Julia flinched and held her breath.

"Mr. Arbeson's trust would certainly cover his debt. What a pity that he doesn't control it. Wouldn't you agree Ms. Metcalf?" He examined Seth's left pinkie finger. "Don't you think that Mr. Arbeson should decide the disposition of what's his?"

Her heart raced faster and she straightened. "No, his family had good reason to…"

The snap of Seth's finger jolted her to the core. She gasped as Seth let loose a scream that grated her spine.

"Perhaps I'm wrong, Ms Metcalf, and you're not as empathetic as I had heard."

"For God's sake, Julia," Seth yelled. "Do whatever he wants."

"Yes, Julia. Do what I want." He ran a hand over her hair. "May I call you Julia? I feel so close to you now."

She tried to muster any courage at all, but the bile rose in her throat despite her efforts.

Noise from above interrupted Albert's train of thought.

"Lon, go see what that is. I need quiet." He stared into Julia's eyes. "I wouldn't want my concentration broken."

Her wide eyes stared back at him as he laughed; his eyes were as soulless as a shark's. Albert's head whipped around as Lon came tumbling back down the stairs.

Albert reached into his jacket and withdrew a pistol. Julia threw her head forward connecting with his arm and sending the pistol clattering over the stones. In a flash of speed, Albert grabbed the knife at his belt as he circled around Julia's chair and held it to the side of her throat.

CHAPTER FIFTY-THREE

"Kitchen's cleared," the agent said quietly. "We haven't cleared the whole house yet, so stay back here, okay?" He disappeared into another part of the house.

"Ten-four," Johnson said. His youthful enthusiasm was close to the surface, but he kept it in check.

Tony, Johnson, and Roark stepped into the kitchen and looked around.

"Wow," Johnson remarked.

It was larger than an apartment and equipped with commercial grade appliances, marble counters, rosewood cabinets and cupboards, and a food preparation area to rival the finest restaurants.

Lange spotted the cellar entrance and pointed. "There it is."

The three drew their weapons and reached for the doorknob. Suddenly, the door opened and Lonny Beck appeared looking very surprised. Tony shoved Beck back, and he tumbled down the stairs.

"Don't move." Johnson yelled as he clambered after him.

Lange and Roark leapt down the stairs and scanned the room with weapons drawn. As they settled into a three-pronged flank, Cordell spoke.

"Welcome, gentlemen. If you don't drop your weapons, I'll slit Ms. Metcalf's lovely throat."

Tony blanched, but kept his weapon leveled on the prim man.

"Let her go," he demanded.

"Please, Officer." Cordell smiled menacingly. "As Mr. Eastwood would say, 'Make my day.'"

"It's Detective."

The gunshot was deafening in the stone room and left Julia's ears ringing. Tony's bullet pierced Cordell's forehead dead center, but the hand that held the razor tensed, and nicked Julia's neck. Lange watched in horror as the blood sprayed.

Time slowed to a crawl. His legs seemed to move in slow motion. Julia's eyes met his briefly before rolling upward. She sagged in the chair. Tony caught her and eased her and the chair to the floor. He pressed his hand firmly onto her jugular and began shouting.

CHAPTER FIFTY-FOUR

THE FEDS CLEARED THE HOUSE QUICKLY and quietly. All the servants had been detained in the pool house. Rogness approached a maid who was wringing her hands and looking around fearfully.

"Where the hell is Hennings?" he demanded.

She shook her head and burst into tears. Rogness rolled his eyes. The police had the cellar covered and it was the only place they hadn't looked. He headed back to the kitchen with the intent of raining on the locals' parade. Cordell was his collar.

As he reached for the cellar door, movement to his right stopped him. As he grasped his weapon, a shoe struck his face with such force that he turned 360 degrees. His fists came up, but way too late. Knuckles moving at a high rate of speed found his nose, and he crumbled to the ground.

Milbert dragged him into the pantry and took Rogness' cap, jacket, and weapon. He slid into the garment with its large FBI identification and pulled the cap down over his eyes.

He peered cautiously though the slightly opened door.

Seeing no one, he slid silently around the corner into the kitchen. A cacophony of voices came from the cellar. He paused at the door to listen. The police shouted, and Mr. Cordell threatened the woman. A shot rang out.

Hennings crept down the stairs. One of the policemen looked in his direction. He nodded and turned toward the action. The ruse worked as the cop turned his attention back to the scene before them.

Cordell's body lay dead on the floor. Anger rose in Hennings until he thought he would burst. He trained the FBI agent's pistol on the center of the second hostage's head. The first lay on the floor in a pool of her own blood.

A lanky detective crouched over her with his hand pressed to her neck while demanding an ambulance. Milbert smiled and shifted his aim to center on Lange's back. His finger tensed on the trigger and he slowly squeezed.

"Freeze!" Johnson yelled.

A deafening sound filled the stone room. Milbert's hand refused to function. He stared at it as it dropped and the stairs rushed up to meet him. His eyes went dull.

Tony glanced over his shoulder to see Milbert staring lifelessly at the ceiling. His gaze shifted to Johnson. He nodded before turning his full attention back to Julia.

"Stay with me, Jule. Come on." Tony held her hand as the medics hurried her out of the cellar and into the waiting ambulance.

"I can't stop the bleeding," one of the paramedics said as the other shut the door then drove off.

Tony ran for his car and jumped in. He turned the key and threw the shifter into DRIVE, squealing the tires to catch up.

JULIA SPED TOWARD A bright light, unable to slow down or comprehend what was happening. Suddenly, she found herself lying back on a blanket staring at the colors of the impending sunset.

Mae sat next to her. It was a beautiful summer evening and her bare toes wiggled in the lawn. "I love how the cool, soft grass feels on my bare feet, don't you, Jule?"

"I like the smell, especially right after it's been cut."

"Look at me, Jule."

Julia sat up and looked Mae in the eye.

"You have to go back. You know that."

Julia heard her name being called from a distance and looked in that direction. She sighed and turned to face her friend. "I know, but I don't want to let go of you."

"You have more to do. You love Tony, and there's a future for the two of you. Don't let that go. It's going be beautiful." Mae smiled, and in a flash of light, she turned into a firefly and flitted off.

"Goodbye, Mae. I love you." Julia turned her head as her name was called again. She got up and started to run toward the sound. Suddenly, she tripped and fell. The dream went black.

"Come on, Jule. Come back to me."

There was such sorrow in Tony's voice that she longed to reach out to him and comfort him. She struggled to the surface and fluttered her eyes.

"Did you see that?" she heard Tony's excited voice say. He sounded like he was in an echo chamber, or maybe under water.

"It may not mean anything." A female voice added.

"I love you, Jule. Don't leave me." His hand squeezed

hers. "You can do it."

"The monitors indicate activity. I'll notify the doctor," the nurse said. There was anticipation in her voice.

The next thing Julia was aware of was pain in her neck, and her mouth was dry.

"Water," she croaked.

Tony's grip on her hand tightened, and she felt hot drops hit her thumb and cool instantly. She opened her eyes with great effort. Tony was holding her hand to his face, tears streaming.

"I thought I was too late. I thought I'd lost you," he said.

She tried to squeeze his hand. "What happened?"

"He cut you when I shot him. Clipped your jugular. You lost a lot of blood." He paused as though gathering himself. "Your heart stopped in the emergency room." He swallowed hard and stabbed a thumb and finger into his eyes. "You were gone for three and a half minutes." It seemed like three and half centuries. He drew in a shaky breath. "I'm so sorry Jule, it was my fault."

She studied his face a moment, seeing the depth of his pain. "You saved me," she said. "*He* cut me." The words were very difficult, and she was exhausted.

The doctor rushed in. He checked her over and asked her some questions she didn't really hear. "Tired," she managed before she passed out again.

"QUIT POKING AT ME," she said as she surfaced again.

"Spunk, I like it." The nurse smiled and busied herself replacing the blood and IV bags then felt Julia's pulse. "We'll need to change your dressing today. Now's as good a time as any since you're awake."

Julia took a look around and saw Tony sleeping uncomfortably in the chair. His face showed several days' growth of beard, and his clothing was rumpled. She touched the nurse's arm. It was far more effort than she anticipated. When the nurse looked her in the eye she asked, "How long have I been here?"

"Three days." She glanced over at Tony. "He's been here since they brought you in, holding your hand every waking moment. He gave blood, too. He wanted to give it several times, since he's the same type as you. We had to tell him we just don't allow that."

Tears spilled over onto Julia's cheeks. She smiled at Tony. At that moment, his eyes fluttered open. He nearly tripped getting out of the chair and over to her bedside.

"Hey," he said tenderly.

"Hey, yourself." She reached up to touch his face.

He simply stared into her eyes for a moment.

"What have I missed?" she whispered.

"Well, the long and short of it is that Cordell is dead, Hennings is dead, and Lon lived to sing like a canary. Seth has been arrested on conspiracy. He'll be waiting a very long time for access to his trust now. It's over, Jule." He leaned in to kiss her.

CHAPTER FIFTY-FIVE

A DREAM HAD HER ONCE AGAIN awaken suddenly. She reached for her journal and quickly scribbled the details. She smiled as she wrote.

I was floating on a cloud over the lake. The waves lapped peacefully on the shore. As I swept downward toward the sandy beach, I could see Mae waving up to me. I leapt off the cloud, and floated to the shore. My feet were moving before they touched the ground. As I met her, I embraced her and kissed her cheek, and my heart sang with delight.

"I'm so happy for you." She clasped both my hands, and began dancing in the sand.

"Why are you so happy, Mae?"

"I'm happy for you, Jule. No one will bother you now. Your decision to set up my foundation was a good one. You're secure without being in danger. I like it."

Mae began to walk down the beach.

"Wait, Mae. Don't go."

"Don't worry Jule. You'll never be alone. Tony will be there."

Mae giggled and ran down the beach. I waved until I could no longer see her.

"Good morning, beautiful." Tony walked in with a breakfast tray, complete with a rosebud in a delicate vase.

"I'm okay, Tony. You don't have to baby me."

"I like babying you."

"Liar." She laughed.

He noticed the journal in her lap. "Did you have another dream?"

"It was about Mae."

"It must've been a good one. It's good to see you smile." His hand trailed down the side of her face."

"It was." She placed her hand over his.

Tony sat on the edge of the bed. "There's something I need to talk to you about." He fidgeted and ran a hand through his hair.

"Oh?"

"I'm just a dumb detective, Jule."

"You're anything but dumb..."

"Let me finish." He drew in an enormous breath and let it all out. "I um... well, I'm just gonna spit it out." He looked away. "I'm dirt poor and you're filthy rich. I'm just an average guy, and you? You're extraordinary. You have a lot of opportunities, Jule. Ones you may not have considered. Or ones you've considered but haven't talked about. Either way, it's not going to be easy for you. I don't want to stand in your way."

What was Tony saying? Her smile disappeared and her chest began to ache. "What are you trying to tell me?" She squeaked out the words.

"Let me finish, please. Like I said, I don't want to stand in your way." His hand covered hers and his eyes captured her gaze. "I want to stand beside you, every step of every moment of our lives. Marry me, Jule."

She blinked; a smile slowly crawled over her face.

"Yes."

He smiled and kissed her softly. From his breast pocket, he produced a lovely antique diamond ring, "This was my mother's."

The journal slid from her lap as she held out her arms to embrace him. "I love you, Tony."

He held her tight for a moment. He slid the ring onto her finger. It fit perfectly, just as his presence fit perfectly in her life. A grin spread across his face as he kissed her hand. His peripheral vision caught something on the open journal page. He picked it up as Julia started to giggle.

"Damn, Mae already told you."

ABOUT THE AUTHOR

C. MERCEDES WILSON is a freelance writer and entrepreneur. She is a member of The Writing and Publishing Group, and Crimescenewriters. Her fascination with writing began early, with a regular column in her junior high school paper, "The Arrow." More recently, she was the winner of the North Hennepin Community College Short Story Contest, 2013. She has a large closely knit family who frequently inspire her work.

Ms. Wilson and her husband live in Fridley, Minnesota with two dogs and a pair of cats who allow them to stay (so far).

ALSO FROM BLUE TULIP PUBLISHING

BY MEGAN BAILEY
There Are No Vampires in this Book

BY J.M. CHALKER
Bound

BY ELISE FABER
Phoenix Rising
Dark Phoenix
From Ashes

BY STEPHANIE FOURNET
Butterfly Ginger

BY JENNIFER RAE GRAVELY
Drown
Rivers

BY E.L. IRWIN
Out of the Blue

BY J.F. JENKINS
The Dark Hour

BY AM JOHNSON
Still Life
Still Water

BY KRISTEN LUCIANI
Nothing Ventured

BY KELLY MARTIN
Betraying Ever After
The Beast of Ravenston

BY NADINE MILLARD
An Unlikely Duchess
Seeking Scandal
The Mysterious Miss Channing

BY LINDA OAKS
Chasing Rainbows

BY C.C. RAVANERA
Dreamweavers

BY GINA SEVANI
Beautifully Damaged

BY ANGELA SCHROEDER
The Second Life of Magnolia Mae
Jade

BY K.S. SMITH & MEGAN C. SMITH
Hourglass
Hourglass Squared
Hourglass Cubed

BY MEGAN C. SMITH
Expired Regrets
Secret Regrets

BY CARRIE THOMAS
Hooked

Secret Dreams

BY K.D. WOOD
Unwilling
Unloved

BOX SET — MULTIPLE AUTHORS
Forbidden
Hurt

www.bluetulippublishing.com